FAMILY

You can pick your friends...

By

Mark Baxter

First published in Great Britain in 2024 by
Mono Media Books (London)
163 A Elmington Road
London SE5 7QZ

ISBN - 978 - 0 - 955557361

A catalogue record for this book is available from the British Library.

This book is dedicated to all those who have stayed close,
but especially to my Lou and Mush xx

I send special love and thanks to the following lovely people.

All those who gave me feedback on an early draft.
You know who you are.

Sharon Purcell – Ta for the proofread cuz x.

David Burke for cracking the code.

Jaymo Kid for the tremendous illustration.

To my agent Rebecca for being there.

And to my old mate Philly Dias for print and design.

CHAPTERS

1.
THE BAKE OFF

Sunlight peeped through a small crack between two curtains and a thin beam of light landed on the face of man fast asleep and snoring gently.
A small brown and white dog got up and stretched its limbs before dropping its body back down on the bed covers and into a nook formed by the legs of the sleeping man who groaned slightly, but who continued sleeping.
Every spare bit of surface of the bedroom was covered with house plants of various greens, punctuated by the occasional pop of colour.
Suddenly a radio alarm clock burst into life. A radio friendly voice with no discernable accent, started to speak in a slightly excited tone of voice.
'Good morning. It's 6am on Saturday 13th April. You're listening to Bosh Radio with me Geoff Spencer. You lucky people. Here is your news at this hour...'
The figure in the bed stirred. He had been distrubed by the voice and was now slowly coming too. He groaned and moaned as he turned and hit the radio as hard as he could, to stop the irratating voice. The silence as he did so was soothing. He began to nod off back to sleep, but a wet sensation on the big toe of his right foot prevented that. He opened one eye and looked down towards his foot. He made a grumbling, earthy sound which stopped the licking, as the small dog recognised, he had caught the man's attention. He then started to speak slowly in a deep, parched, weary voice.

'Alright…alright…fuck ya… I know…'
The man threw back the covers and looked at the clock, still only using the one eye.

‘Can’t be?’
There was more groaning heard as he slowly shifted to the edge of the bed. He sat there for a few seconds, and rubbed his face, trying to get his bearings. He was in his late 60s and his face hadn’t been anywhere near a razor for a few days. He was wearing a shapeless white – ish vest and blue and white striped boxer shorts. A couple of now fading blue/black tattoos could be seen on his hands. He also had a reddish coloured sock on his left foot. The small dog excitedly jumped up towards him, wagging its small tail 20 to the dozen and panting happily as it did so.

‘Steady Daisy girl, yeh mate, yeah morning....I’m coming, I’m flaming coming…’
The man stood up and looked around for yesterday’s clothes which were lying on the floor exactly where he left them the night before, as he got undresed to get into bed.
‘Sock? Where’s me other…’
Daisy having got off the bed briefly, had now returned with the ‘other’ sock, between her jaws. The man cleared his throat and said lightly…
‘Gis it Daise, go on, gis it then…’
Daisy sensed it was play time and began to wag her tail and joyfully shake the sock about, with no intention of letting it go.
‘Give me, the flipping, sock mate…’
This was said in a slightly harder tone. His patience was now wearing thin. He made a grab for the sock and Daisy immediately began to pull in the opposite direction.
‘Fuck me girl…You’re stopping yourself going out aintcha?’
The slight anger in his voice, froze Daisy. The man now had hold of her bottom jaw and he gently eased her mouth open, managing to free the now damp, soggy, shapeless sock. He then slowly pulled it over his right foot.
‘Thank you for that kind gesture, much appreciated I’m sure.’

He couldn't help but smile as he gently rubbed Daisy's head and continued getting dressed, pulling on his baggy, saggy, grey jogging bottoms. Next, he slipped on a pair of scuffed off-white Reebok trainers and tucked the laces down inside of the shoe, not bothering to tie them. He then threw on and zipped up, a navy coloured puffa coat over his vest.
He shuffled into his bathroom and the sound of him having a wee, made Daisy look his way, sensing the time for a walk was nigh.
Our man then walked towards his front door. He stopped and kissed two fingers, and without looking, placed them on a photo of a young woman on the wall. To the side of the door, he took a dog lead off the hook where it lived and clipped it to Daisy's collar. He then collected a tartan shopping trolley from his kitchen, tied the dog by its lead to it and then left his flat through the front door.

The estate lift delivered him to ground level and he emerged from the main security door to his block, beginning a slow walk towards a parade of shops. As he neared a well-worn grassy area, he slipped Daisy off her lead and she ran over quickly to the nearest lampost, squatted and peed.
The man looked down at his dog, as if it was a small child.
'Done? You sure? Come here then. There's a good girl.'
He reached into the right pocket of his puffa coat and found a small piece of dog biscuit, which he then gave to Daisy. She gently took it from his fingers and quickly crunched it into oblivion. He then clipped her back on her lead. He let out a small groan as he straightened up and continued his walk toward the shops.

As he did so, ahead of him, he noticed two figures coming his way. He made a grumbling, annoyed noise as he got a few feet from them.

‘Oi oi! Here’s an early riser. Alright Terry?
Terry nodded towards them, and then split them up by walking between them, so each man ended up either side of him
‘Alright Patsy… Del...’
‘Nice set of wheels you got there Tel boy.’
Terry stopped walking and turned to look at Patsy.
‘Bit early for you two plums innit Pats?’
Del looked excitedly at Terry
‘Just getting in, innit mate. Poker night down at Muzzy’s. Nicked a nice few quid as it happens, had a right result…’
Terry held up his right hand, stopping Del in mid flow, feeling irritated.
‘Listen, Del. Sorry like, but can’t stop and listen to your no doubt, riveting gambling tales, cos if I don’t get my rolls by 6.30, Guray will sell out and I won’t be a happy camper, you get me?
Terry stared him down and Del looked towards the pavement.
‘You mind how you go Del…’

Terry began to walk again, Daisy now pulling him towards the shops.
‘Rolls? Flipping rolls. Can’t have that can we mate? You know Del, it’s funny, cos the people round here used to warn me about him.’
Patsy was smiling, as he nodded towards Terry.
Terry was now standing still with his back to Del and Patsy. His face was now a mixture of anger and pity. Patsy then continued.
‘Oh yeh, he was a right tearaway on the manor I heard. One of the chaps, they reckon.’
As he’s talking, Patsy was looking at Terry’s red and black tartan, shopping trolley.

'Though, I bet he didn't have one of them in the boot of his getaway motor.'
Del started laughing and even Terry raised a smile as Patsy carried on talking.
'Got to say though, suits him now, eh?
Terry turned very slowly and looked at them both, still smiling and now shaking his head.

'You finished have ya? Had your giggle? All that was a long time ago boys. Another lifetime. Now, if you don't mind...'
He looked at them both directly in their eyes, which forced Del to once again, look at the floor.
'I've got an appointment. Come on Daisy, and bollocks to ya, you pair of plums... '
He turned away from them again and groaned to himself as he walked away, leaving them laughing and pointing at him.

Terry eventually arrived outside the Turkish bakers he'd been aiming at since he left his flat. He peered in through the steamed-up shop window and saw Guray pulling hot grey metal trays of rolls and bread out of fierce looking hot ovens and then leaving them to cool down. Terry entered the shop, dragging a reluctant Daisy in with him. Guray was dressed in all white, with white crocs on his white towelling sock covered feet. He even had white flour all mixed in with his already greying hair. He'd been baking since 2am, getting his orders ready and there was now loose flour covering every stainless-steel surface as far as the eye could see.
'That dog has never liked this shop, has she?' said Guray in his own distinctive London/Turkish accent, all the while smiling at Daisy.
'Think it's your aftershave son.' laughed Terry
'Bit late today Tel. I was beginning to think you were going to give it a miss for the first time in years.'

Terry smiled at the baker.
'Perish the thought, No, I ran into a couple of right nuisances, intent on wasting my valuable time. Pair of comedians. Well, they made themselves laugh.
Got my coupla bits ready for me then?'
Guray smiled at his old friend.
'Course, no dramas. Usual I take it?'
Terry nodded. Guray turned and started putting Terry's order together, pulling rolls and bread and cakes from the various trays and tins around the shop and putting them into white paper bags of various sizes.
'Right there you go. Dozen rolls, 3 cut loaves, couple of bits of bread pudding and I put your spare bags in there too.'
'Blinding. You're a good man G.'
Terry paid Guray and then loaded up his shopping trolley.
'Thanks mate, can't beat a drop of hot bread can ya? These smell lovely and fresh. Now you get home you and put those feet up.'
'Im listening. Quick tidy up and will do. Mind how you go Tel, and you too Daisy. Keep well son and see you next week.'
Terry, halfway out of the shop door, slowed and looked back.
'If spared tosher, if spared.'

2.
LOVE THY NEIGHBOUR

His bakery mission now completed; Terry headed back towards his estate. His next stop was Amin's Newsagent, where Terry stocked up on various newspapers. These too were safely ensconced into his shopping trolley, and he and Daisy slowly meandered home. Terry got in the lift and headed up towards the first floor. Once there, he carefully took out 4 bread rolls from his shopping trolley and put them into one of his spare paper bags. He added a loaf to that, plus a copy of The Sun newspaper. He then walked to the left of the landing and pressed the doorbell at flat number 4. There was no immediate sign of anyone in, but finally he could hear some shuffling about, and the flat door was then opened by a small woman in her mid 60s. She had a bright blonde rinse in her hair, and wore a reddish velvet looking hoodie and leggings combination, with fake diamonds running down the sleeves and legs.

'Morning Else. You alright girl? There ya, go...'
Terry began handing over his delivery, though he was somewhat blinded by the bling that was shining back his way.
'You're a lovely man Terry, and yes I'm fine ta. You alright mate?'
Her voice was pure old South East London. Elsie then looked down at Terry's feet.
'ello little Daisy, ah bless 'er…'
Terry didn't immediately answer, still somewhat spellbound by Elsie's outfit.
'What you looking at?' asked Elsie, looking down at her clothing.
'This?' My granddaughter Cherish bought it for me last Christmas. Dontcha like it Tel? Love them diamonds me.'

'Eh? No, it's er, great.'
'Good girl she is. Treating me to have lip fillers next week, bless her.'
Elsie then took some loose change from her purse and handed over the right amount of money.
'Think you'll find that correct love.'
Terry had a quick look at the coins in his hands.
'That's spot on Else. Ok, better crack on love. You look after yourself mate, you hear? And go easy on your lips. All you girls end up looking a bleeding goldfish.'
Elsie laughed, as she mimed puffing her lips out.
'Ta la Tel, I will mate.'

Terry's next stop was flat number 8, one flight up. Terry rapped the door knocker twice and not long after it was slowly opened by a thin man in his late 30s. His head was wrapped in a turban made from a bath towel and he was wearing a silky burgundy and bright pink floral dressing gown. A Scouse accent as thick as a bacon sandwich served up in Maries café, on the Walworth Road, greeted Terry.
'Morning Terence, you're looking radiant this morning love.'
The emphasis on the word radiant, saw Terry smile shyly.
'Behave yourself you. Everything ok with you Dolly. I thought I heard some shouting up here last night?'
Dolly looked confused.
'Eh? No don't think so? Oh, hang on, that was the caveman next door, giving me some verbals. Fair to say, he's not a lover of my tribe him. All piss and wind him though. Nothing to worry about there.'
Terry nodded.
'Charming. Listen if he carries on, you tell me…'
'Don't worry Terry love. Goes with the landscape. I can handle him. Anyway, think he secretly fancies me. Now give me my vittles you lovely man.'

Terry smiled as he handed over 4 rolls, a loaf of bread and a copy of The Guardian.
'Terry, hate to ask, but can you put it on the slate? Theres a love. Settle next week. Promise...'
A pained look came over Terry's face. He also did his best to look angry, but it wasn't really working.

'Now don't come it Doll. You owe me two weeks already mate.'
'Ah, I know I do petal, but I've picked up a week in The Clyde from tonight, doing my 'Dusty' so I'll sort you out after that. Ah, go on Terry love...'
'Not happy Dolly. Wont lie. You're taking advantage of me you are.'
Dolly broke out into a mischevious grin.
'Just give me half a chance love, that is all I'm saying.'
Terry smiled again, though he tried hard not to.
'Murder you are...Ok, next week, but no messin', you hear me?'
Dolly blew him a big kiss and then quickly turned and shut his front door, laughing as he did so.

Terry's last drop was at number 12 and Gloria who lived there, was waiting for him as he finally arrived. Her and Terry had shared a landing for many years, pretty much since she arrived from Jamaica in the late 1970s.
She broke out into a broad smile as soon as she saw him.
'Oh, here he is, blessings upon you. We give thanks. The kettles on, got time for a cuppa love?'
Terry smiled as he heard Gloria's voice.
'Ta Gloria, but better not. Need to feed Daisy and I badly need a pony mate. Besides, the boy wonder will be round at 11. Can't keep royalty waiting, can we?'

Gloria laughed out loud, as she handed over the money for her loaf and paper.
'There's a little extra there, to get Daisy a little chew or something.'
'Ah, thats very sweet of you Glor, very thoughtful. Hear that Daise? Gloria treated ya.'
Daisy jumped up at Terry's legs at the sound of her name being mentioned, causing her owner to slightly lose his balance.
'Steady girl, steady, nearly had me over there.'
'That dog doesn't miss much, does she? Alright then if you are sure. See you later Terry.'
Gloria turned and shut the front door behind her.

Terry walked a few paces to his right, and towards his own flat, number 11.
On the way, he absent-mindely deadheaded a few pansies from the many window boxes on his part of the landing, before unlocking the door of his own flat, and taking himself and Daisy home.

3.
BLOOD IS THICKER THAN MUD

A gleaming black, chauffeur driven Daimler drove onto the litter strewn estate and parked up. A mixed-race man in his mid to late 40s emerged from the back seats. He wore all black designer clothing, complete with black trainers with gleaming white soles. Despite it being overcast above, he also wore sunglasses. As he walked towards the entry door of the block he wanted, he looked around the estate and shook his head as if pitying the place.
He then pressed the button for number 11 on the intercom. A crackling noise was heard which the man in black responded to.
'Hello uncle, its me.'

He exited the lift on the 4th floor and pressed the doorbell to Terry's flat. Gloria emerged carrying a black plastic bag full of household rubbish, which she threw down the communal chute to the large refuse bin below.
'Oh, hello Darren, I mean Ryan. Sorry, Mr Williams. Just putting some rubbish in the…I saw you on the telly last week. Very good that I thought... '
Darren looked her way. Sunglasses still in place
'Hello Mrs. Dyer, that's very kind of you to say so. Please, just call me Darren. You all good?'
Gloria nodded and then just looked at him, smiling, but not speaking.
Darren looked back at Terry's front door for a few seconds and then back at Gloria, who was still smiling at him. Both are now lost, not knowing what to say next. Darren pressed the doorbell again.

An awkward silence remained for a further 5 seconds, which felt like a lot longer to both of them. Finally, the door opened, and Darren quickly walked in. In his haste, he brushed past Terry, who was holding a green plastic watering can.

'Alright Dal? Whats up? You got the hump already? Only just got here... '
Once inside, Darren slowly removed his sunglasses.
'Bit weird out there with Mrs. Dyer. She came out, having a nose... '
Terry had followed his nephew indoors.
'Who my Gloria? Weird? Nah. She's alright, Its your fault. Not used to seeing you on her telly thats all. Known you since a nipper, so got to be odd that, you now popping up on there every 5 minutes.'
Darren looked back at Terry unconvinced.
'Listen, you're a bit of glamour aint ya? She's got fuck all else to look forward to, day in, day out. I think you should be pleased she came out, personally.'
Terry continued on his walk round the flat, watering the odd house plant here and there as he goes by on his way to the kitchen.
'Made you a ham roll. Bread pudding for afters...'
Darren nodded.
'Nice, thank you. Listen, I am pleased she's watched my stuff unc, and I like Mrs. Dyer, I really do. It's just very, very awkward, sometimes. She even called me Darren, then Ryan, then Mr Williams.'

'Well, thats your own fault that is. One minute, you're little snotty nosed Darren living on here with my Tricia. Then suddenly you're Ryan Williams the AC-TOR. I mean, it is odd, seeing my sister's kid in the films and that. That's what other people do.'

Darren was only half listening, finding his mind wandering back to his years living on the estate. He smiled as he saw himself playing football between the garages and then suddenly, that smile turned to a frown, as he saw himself, then aged about 15, surrounded by by a gang of older boys, all wearing the same gang name on their hooded tops, saying The Awakening. They are shoving bags of weed and pills his way and he saw himself shaking his head. One of the gang, the leader, is really threatening Darren, and has his left hand around Darren's neck, his right hand pointing a large kitchen knife towards Darren's throat, whilst pinning him to the ground.
'See these? Take them and deliver them to a name I'm gonna give ya.'
Darren saw himself struggle and shake his head, doing his best to get out of the situation he found himself in.
'Don't disappoint me. Make an enemy of me and you know you'll regret it. Do it. I said, do it!'
Darren struggled with all his might but felt that that was hopeless, and he is losing the battle.
'This is no polite request, d'ya get me?'
Darren is then slapped and punched repeatedly in his face and body, first by the leader and then by the others in the gang. He saw himself cowering on the floor, covering up the best he could.

'What you want, tea or coffee? Dal..Darren!'
Darren startled, jumped slightly as the flashback running in his mind ended abruptly.
'Eh? Er, coffee, black. Sorry, heavy night. Where was I? Oh yeh, long time ago all that unc? All moved on. Well, some of us have.'

Within 5 minutes,Terry came in from the kitchen, carrying a tray with his and Darren's lunch on it. He placed that down on

a tiled topped coffee table, finding space in between a couple of house plants on either side. He then handed a mug of coffee to Darren.
'Listen, you might have moved on son, but many on here aint gone nowhere.'
Terry slowly walked over to a window and pulled the white net curtains to one side.
'Turned up in the big motor again I see.'
'What? Yeh well, on the way to see Moira about a new offer. Was re-reading my bit of the script in the back. Handy having Simon driving today. Two birds, one stone.'
Terry sniffed and looks unconvinced.
'I guess so... Could look a bit poncey though mate.'
Darren looked quizzically at Terry.
'Poncey? How?'
Terry looked pityingly back at his nephew.
'What d'ya mean how? Alright you're doing well, but turning up in a big motor like that, when most on here aint got two bob for the gas man, I mean…'

Darren rubbed his forehead, like he was massaging away a headache.
'Don't start Terry, please. I mean, I aint trying to rub anyones nose in anything am I? Practical, that's all. Moira wanted me genned up for this new action hero part which I start training for on Monday and I wanted to see you. Got both done by having the motor.'
Terry sat down in his armchair and grabbed his plate of food from the coffee table.
'I aint starting. What part, what training?'
Darren sat down and was now directly facing Terry.
'For this new film. I'm going in a boxing gym for a couple of months. Got to get fitter and learn how to punch properly… Listen, you want me to get Simon to move the car?'

Terry is mid bite but shakes his head, his mouth now full of food.
'No, you plum, I was just saying.'
'I know you were just saying unc, but what do you want me to do. Come by poxy bus?
'Oh, do leave off.'
'Ok, I hear ya Terry. Listen, it is what it is. Anyway, I want to have my roll and a cuppa with you. Bollocks to everyone else. Making sure you're ok, that's all Im doing.'
Terry smiled at Darren, who also now had a mouthful of ham roll.
'I know son, I know. Listen, you know how proud of you I am, and I'm always delighted to see you, anytime. I know you're busy...'
Darren looked lovingly at his uncle.
'Love ya unc. You know I'll always be grateful. Always...'
Terry puts his right index finger to his lips.
'Sshhh boy, sshhh... No need for any of that. Family son. What we do innit? Now eat your flaming grub.'

4.
WELL, HELLO DOLLY

It's a few days later, and Terry emerged from his block to take Daisy for her evening walk. Feeling the fine rain hitting him in the face, he pulled up the hood of his puffa coat over his head with his free hand. The pair walk towards a well trodden path on the main grass area which surrounded the estate and then onto the main pavement by the parade of shops. Almost immediately Terry noticed a group of six to eight people looking at something on the ground by the bus stop, some fifty yards or so in front of him.

As he got closer, Terry noticed it was actually a woman on the pavement, which the crowd were all looking at. She was slumped there, with part of her back resting on the graffiti covered brick wall behind her. Terry caught the eye of a man in among the small crowd. The man nodded to Terry and began to talk, but never once took his eye off of the woman.
'Bird been mugged I reckon. Shocking innit? Won't have an ambulance called though. I did ask.'
Terry looked down at the blonde-haired woman. She had a big imitation fur coat wrapped around her shoulders and her gold lame dress sparkled in the light rain, flood lit by the streetlamp she was directly under. One of her white, high heeled shoes, lay on its side a few feet from her. The other one was just about still in place, on her left foot. The woman kept her head down, not looking at anyone in the crowd. Terry was now seriously staring at the woman, with a very quizzical look on his face.
'Doll? Dolly...that you?
The woman looked up at him. She had a large fiery red mark on her left cheek. Her mascara had now met the rain and black streaks had run down her face. She then shut her eyes, trying

to somehow keep the embarrassment and pain that she was now feeling, as far away as possible.

With a heavy sigh, Dolly began to speak.
'Hello Tel. Yeh, it's me love...'
Recognising the voice, Daisy ambled over to Dolly and licked his hand. Dolly slowly smiled.
'Hello Daisy girl.'
The male onlooker who first spoke to Terry spotted a quick getaway.
'Know her do ya?'
Terry ignored him.
'What the fuck happened Dolly?
The man persisted.
'Cos if you do, I'll leave you with her. My bus is coming. Want to get home for the highlights.'
Terry looked at him, suddenly realising he was being talked to.
'Yeh, yeh. I know her. Go on, you crack on mate. Actually, all of ya. Bless ya's. Please, go. Its alright. She'll be fine. Thanks for your help.'
The crowd around Dolly, slowly dispersed, until just Dolly, Terry and Daisy were left.
Terry leaned down towards Dolly
'Right, gis your arm, let's get you up off that wet floor.'
He extended his right arm towards Dolly, who grabbed it and Terry pulled him up. Dolly stumbled a bit, as Terry put his left arm around his waist. Still wearing just the one shoe, Dolly made a few small groaning noises as he rose to his feet. Once steady, he put the loose shoe back on, wincing as he did so.
'Flaming Ada. I had a right bump on landing there.'
Terry stared at Dolly, his face full of questions
'So wha'...?'
Dolly slowly shook his head.
'Not here love. Get me home first Terry, eh?

5.
THAT WAS YOUR LIFE

Dolly limped towards the front room of his flat, with the sound of a flushed toilet heard in the background. The wig, dress, fur coat and shoes had all gone and been replaced by a white towelling dressing gown. The new look was completed by a white towel wrapped round his head. Only the bright red nail varnish on his fingers and toes remained. Dolly smiled as he noticed two nails, one from each hand, had been lost in the fall earlier.

As he entered his front room, he also noticed Daisy fast asleep directly under a radiator. About to sit down, he spied Terry looking confused, standing in the doorway of the kitchen.

'What's up Terry love?'

'Can't find the flaming coffee, can I?'

'Top shelf, above the sink. Might be at the back? And chuck us a ciggy, will ya please Tel. They're in there somewhere'

Terry quickly looked around and then picked up a packet of 20 Benson from the work top near to the kettle. He then returned to the front room.

'Ready? Here y'are'

He gently lobbed the fags towards Dolly who caught them carefully. He then took a purple plastic coloured lighter from his dressing gown pocket and sparked the end of one of the cigarettes into life.

Terry then returned to the kitchen, to resume his search of the coffee.

'Coffee... coffee…ah, there ya are ya little fucker!'

Dolly hobbled over to a set of shelves and picked up a newly opened bottle of scotch. Terry re-entered the room, with a couple of cups, sugar bowl and spoons set out on a tray.

'Brought the milk, sugar an' that. Not sure how you like it?
Dolly smiled at him.
'Well, I'll have a drop of this in it for a flaming kickoff...'

Dolly sat down on a beige fabric armchair and opened the bottle and poured out a decent glug into his cup of coffee. He then held up the bottle up to Terry.
'Go on then. Keep that chill off my chesticles...'
Terry smiled as he then poured a small amount in his coffee and he settled down on the nearby matching settee. A silence descended over them, as they looked at each other and then Terry glanced at the fixtures and fittings of the room.
'Nice wall colouring and love the rugs. All very tastefully, er, decorated...'

By now the silence between the two was deafening and Terry could stand it no longer.
'Listen, I won't ask if you don't want me to, but...'
Dolly looked him straight in the eye.
'You're a good man Terry. Always known that.'
Terry smiled and looked down into his coffee. He was not used to compliments and had no experience in knowing how to accept them. Dolly continued.
'But I'm in no mood to go into what happened tonight. Let's just say I walked into someone I shouldn't have...'
The smile on Terry's face suddenly faded. He looked at the angry red mark on Dolly's face.
'Right, right...and what, they did that, did they?'
'Just told ya, leave it Terry. Goes with the territory love...'
'I'm sorry Doll. Not really my nature to leave it. Especially stuff like this. Hate anything like this...'
Dolly sighed
'Like what Terry? What do you think you are seeing, eh?'
Terry momentarliy looked confused.

'Bullying. Intimidation. Gonna be something like that innit?'

Dolly took a hefty drag on his cigarette and blew a plume of greyish/blue smoke towards his white ceiling.
'This is the result of what they now call homophobic abuse. Queer bashing in your day love. You, are now looking at a victim of that.'
Terry looked down at the carpet, not sure what to say.
'The only reason I got a clump tonight was because I'm gay Terry. I mean, a bloke walking around in a gold cocktail dress might make some people think that, but then most people, thankfully, don't then give that bloke a right-hander for doing so.'
Terry's face began to glow, a combination of the scotch finding its sweet spot, and general anger beginning to rise up inside him.

'Listen, I can hear you have had enough for one night Doll, and that's fair enough, but just tell me if you know who did it and then leave it to me.'
Dolly took another deep intake of his cigarette.
'Had a great night. I had sung really well, third night running going down a storm at The Clyde. The punters loved my Dusty. Then I had a drink or three after I finished and well, you know, got brave. So, I walked home in my finery instead of getting changed back into my jeans and that. Only, I then walked into someone who obviously preferred Lulu?'

Terry shook his head slowly.
'Nah, I'm not having it.'
Dolly looked at him in disbelief.
'What d'ya mean, you're not having it? Not about you though love, is it? Us who live like we do, are used to this sweetheart. It's what happens Terry. All the fucking time. In this so called

enlightened era, we are supposed to be living in, there are still cavemen out there, who ain't got the memo, know worra mean?'
Terry looked up at the word cavemen and nodded.

'No, you're right. Sorry Doll. Lost me rag. I've always had a bad temper. Bit of a trait of mine you could say, well certainly used to be. I simply hate injustice of any kind, always have.'
Dolly looked lovingly at Terry.
'Bless your heart, and I mean that, but you can't fight all the worlds battles can ya love? Especially mine. You'd be putting in for overtime with me. Listen, I'll be alright. Bit of an achey face in the morning and a sore bum for a few days where I landed but won't be the first time, I've had that…Sorry. Couldn't resist.'
Terry went a brighter shade of red.
'Are you blushing Terence?'
'Me? Nah, it's that scotch hitting home.'
Terry nodded towards the bottle.
'In truth, it's not the fire water that brings up the anger Doll. It's all a bit deeper than that. Goes back to when I was a teenager. Something happened, that changed me. Left me with a lot of anger. It just surfaces from time to time.'

Dolly smiled at him.
'Well, as we're in the confession box...'
Terry looked at Dolly and smiled.
'Nah, all a long time ago Doll.'
'Bollocks. Come on, Jackanory with Terry time.'
Terry smiled and took a glug of his drink.
'Alright, only fair I s'pose...'
He filled his cup with more scotch and then took another decent slurp. He then settled further back into the settee.
'You know, I worked out by the time I was coming up to 23,

24, that the only way I would get what I wanted out of life, y'know a few quid, gaff of my own, nice motor, all that which is supposed to bring us happiness, was to go on the rob. I mean, I could see no other way. I'd left school with cough all. Nothing. Even my blazer didn't fit me anymore. I tried a couple jobs for a couple of years, but in all that time, I just earnt enough to pay my old girl some rent and have enough for a pint or two or take a girl to the pictures, but not both. It was alright for a while, but I soon wanted more.'

Dolly lit up another fag and looked intently at Terry.
'Same as us all love, it's just our lot in life isn't it? Never had any spare money. Have to get grafting as soon as we can?'
Terry sipped his drink.
'Yeh, and we are supposed to accept that, but I don't know Doll. I kept thinking, that there had got to be more to it than what I ended up with. Then I met a girl. Margaret, everyone called her Peggy, out of Kennington.'
'Oh, hang on, young love enters the film!'
Terry couldn't help but smile.
'Yep, and it was exactly that Dolly. Love. And I was all in. I admit, I really loved her, the first time I felt like that. And so, I wanted to give her the best. She said, all she wanted, was me. Only, I wasn't listening. I wanted her to have more.

Terry picked up the bottle of scotch and topped up his cup. His telling of the story was slowly getting faster and faster. It felt good to get it off his chest and that scotch tasted good.
'Then, word reached me, of a tickle with a firm. Fella I knew was looking for another pair of hands, but this was proper villainy, and a real earner. Yes, I felt the risk, but I promised myself I'd do the one job, earn some dough and then get out. Anyway, it was a security van blag. The firm were short of a driver. I told them I was a wheel man. They had doubts, but

:e in need, so...'

ıt there engrossed. Ash from his fag fell directly onto ... sing gown without being noticed.

'On the day, the security chaps handed over the gelt, with no thoughts of being a hero, especially with a sawn off being waved under their noses. It was all done in seconds and then it was down to me. I went toe down, and bosh, away, job done. No sign of the old bill. Clean away. My share came to 10 grand.

Dolly grinned.

'Decent money that back then I bet?'

'Very decent Doll. Splashed a bit of the dough on Peggy straight away. New frocks, nights up West, all the trimmings. I was Jack, the bleedin', lad…'

They both smiled at what that comment conjured up.

'I was then offered more work with the chaps, but I said no, I'm out. Truth is, they didn't like that, I guess it left them feeling nervous, but I was done. That one job had proved villainy was not for me. I really hated being involved. Even the money I was spending felt dirty. I knew that game was not for me. Then I heard in a pub that the same firm turned over a bank two weeks later, again with shooters being waved about.'

Terry drained his coffee cup, and his gaze drifted off into the middle distance.

'Then, it all came on top. Old bill pulled in the top man from my one. Someone had grassed him to the local plod. The guv'nor on that squad was known for taking a back hander, well, they all did then. Told our man he'd cock a deaf 'un for a nice drink. So, the top man paid him a coupla grand. But then the copper came back and then demanded someone had to go in the frame for a job after all. Apparently, those above the crooked one, were screaming blue murder, because guns were used. They needed a name to go down for it. By the look on your face Dolly, you've guessed the rest...'

Dolly now had his head in his hands. A look of shock all over his now bruised face.
'No, no, no. They never…'
Terry just nodded at him.
'The truth is Doll, you can never really leave it, the way I tried to. One job gets your card marked. So, they stuck my name up. I was stitched up and I went away for the job I wouldn't do. They got a message to me saying 'nothing personal Tel' and promised me I'd be looked after when I got out, but they turned me right over. But the truth is Dolly, ultimately my greed was to blame.'
Dolly topped up his cup and went in search of another fag.
'Bloody hell Terence…How long d'ya get?"
'Fifteen-year. All down to the use of the firearms. As I was the only one caught, they made an example of me. Because I was only the driver, I was told I would be out around ten if I kept my head down. My Peggy wrote a couple of times at first and then that stopped. Didn't blame her. Poor mare was only 20. Had her whole life in front of her. I'd fucked it right up. Then I got angry. Mainly with myself, for being so dense, but also those around me, who let me walk right into it. Honour among thieves they say, don't they? Do me a favour.'

A silence descended between the two men, as each reflected on the tale so far.
'Still, I never grassed, but fuck me, I did get bitter and a raging anger surfaced that has never really left me in truth. You saw a bit of that earlier. That fire will never go out, not until I turn my toes up.'
'Well. You've always been a bit of a mystery, but I didn't see any of that coming.'
'There's nothing mysterious about me Doll, not really. It was

all about trust when I got out, and in truth, I trusted no one. I just keep myself to myself. To this day, I just want to be left alone. Honestly, I had enough of people a long time ago. Plums most of 'em, present company excluded of course...'
Dolly got up and curtsied, and then quickly remembered his aching bones.
Terry laughed and then looked lovingly at Daisy, still fast asleep over by the radiator.
'That dog over there and my plants do me. I know where I am with them. Apart from that, I only let a very few good people in, and when I do,I try to look after them as best I can. That's why tonight hurt me, because you are one of 'em.'

Dolly got up from his chair and slowly limped over to Terry and kissed him on his head.
'Come on you. Enough excitement for one night, for both of us as it happens. Home now and take little Daisy with ya, or we'll have the neighbours gossiping and my reputation will be in tatters'
Terry looked at Dolly and smiled.
'Well, we can't have that, can we Dusty love? '

6.
A FLAME THAT NEVER DIED

Terry is sat in his favourite brown leather armchair, his feet raised up on a battered old brown corduroy pouffe. He had a large glass of red wine with his right hand balanced on the arm of the chair, He was watching an old episode of Minder on his telly and his eyes are getting steadily heavier as he slowly fell asleep.

Suddenly, his mobile phone, which had fallen into his lap, burst into life. Terry woke up with a start and spilt a little of the red wine onto the chair.
'Bollocks! Fucks sake…'
He fumbled for the phone with his left hand, as he clumsily tried to put the glass down on his front room carpet. He opened the leather effect flap of the protective cover wrapped around his phone and looked for a name on its screen, over the top of his glasses. It read 'private number.'
'Oh, do fuck off…'
He instantly killed the call.
'Poxy scam merchants.'
He then blindly reached down for his wine glass and carefully found its rim, which he pinched between his thumb and index finger and gently hoisted it back into its previous position.
Twenty seconds later, the phone rang again. Once again, Terry looked at its screen. Once again, he saw 'private number' and once again he instantly killed the call.
Within ten seconds, it rung again.
Anger had now swelled up inside Terry as this time, he pressed the green button to accept the call.
'Listen, you plums, whoever you are. Fuck off with your nonsense, I'm…'

His rant was interrupted by a soft female voice which suddenly spoke into his right ear.
'Terry...that you? Hello… Terry...?
With a look of total surprise all over his face, Terry now held up the phone and looked in vain for a name. Once again, all he saw was 'private number.'
He put the phone back to his ear.
'Who's that?
'Terry? Is that you?
'Saying nothing, til I know who this is.'
'I'm looking to speak to Terry, Terry Williams?
The original look of surprise on his face, had now been replaced by one of intrigue.
'Hold on, hold on, gotta turn me telly down.'
He pointed his remote control at Arthur Daley and hit the mute button.
'Right. Yeh, this is Terry Williams. Who's this?'
There then began an edgy silence. Terry's eyes darted from side to side, as he listened intently, trying to pick up clues as to who was on the other end. Finally, the voice returned.
'It's me…Peggy...'

Terry's mind frantically searched under P, trying to find a match.
'Peggy? Peggy who? Don't know anyone called…'
Slowly a look of 'can't be' spread all over his face.
'Hang on, hang on. You mean, Peggy, as in from…you know...'
'Yeah, that one. Me... your old Peggy...'
It was now Terry's turn to fall silent. He opened his mouth a couple of times, but in truth he was at a loss as to anything sensible to say.
'Fuck me...'
He heard gentle laughter coming down the phone back to him.

'I'm sorry for swearing, only…'
The smile in Peggy's voice can be heard as she spoke.
'It's me who should be saying sorry Terry. I've startled you.'
'Er, well yeh, you have a bit. How did you, y'know, my number?
'Long story. Listen, I hope you don't mind me calling. Not sure I should of now...'
'No, no. Its alright, really. Just a big surprise, thats all...'

'Well, I read an article in a magazine about the actor, Ryan Williams.'
A quizzical look came over Terry's face.
'Him? What's he got to do with…
'Ssshh will ya. Let me finish. Anyway, this Ryan…'
'You know thats my Darren dontcha, my nephew? I still call him by his real name, me...'
'TERRY! For gawds sake, this aint easy for me, so let me talk please. I'm getting all flustered here.'
Terry smiled as he heard the defiance in her voice.
'Sorry Peg.'
She then began to tell her story really quickly, so quickly in fact, that Terry struggled to hear everything she said.
'Anyway, in the article, that Ryan said he was out of Lambeth and his uncle Terry had paid for him get to drama school. He said without that, he'd probably be inside or worse, because he was going down a bad path as a teenager. I thought can't be. Terry Williams? Lambeth? About the right age an' that.'
Terry's face was all screwed up as he tried to make sense of what he was hearing.
'Blimey. I only caught half of that. You need to slow down girl.'
'Sorry, me nerves aint it, shaking like a leaf here.'
'Well, yeh, that was me. I saw it as helping my kid sister Tricia really. Darren is her boy. '

Peggy smiled at the memory of her name.
'Ah, I remember Tricia, always nice to me she was.'
Terry nodded as a sad look came over his face.
'She was a good kid. One of the best. When I came out from the nick, and was back on the estate, I found her pregnant, with no bloke about. A bit of a shock that. To be honest I was no use to her as I got on the drink heavy. Trying to drown my sorrows I guess? Anyway, I was bang on it for a good few year.'
Peggy fell silent for a few seconds
'You said was then...'
'Eh?'
'When you mentioned Tricia, you said was...'
'Oh, you wouldn't know would ya? Yeh, she died the poor mare. A few years back now. Never that strong. She got on the drink too. I tried to help, but as I said....'
'Oh, I am sorry to hear that. Really liked her.'
'It was a terrible time Peg. Anyway, when she was gone, her fella at the time, Clive, nice bloke, asked me to help with Darren, who would have been about fourteen then. Almost overnight, I packed up the booze, or at least got it under better control. That boy was always going to come first in whatever I did from then on.'
Peggy dropped her voice to almost a whisper.
'You were always kind...'

'Eh? Well, not sure about any of that. Anyway. My number?
Peggy laughed gently at the discomfort she could hear in Terry's voice.
'So, I Googled Ryan Williams and found a contact for his agent. I emailed them and said who I was and that I think I knew Ryan's uncle years ago and did they have a contact for him, please. To be honest, I thought I was wasting my time, and it went quiet for a fortnight or so. Then ping, I got a reply from a woman called Moira, telling me Ryan had read

my email and said to pass on your number.'
'The flaming cow'son!'
'Now, Terry! Don't be like that.'
'Well, I just wish he had told me'
'To be honest, I wasn't sure I was even going to call.'
Terry couldn't help but laugh out loud.
'Ha! This gets better and better. Charming that is...'
Peggy also let out a gentle laugh.
'Oi you, behave. You know what I mean you sod.'

'Listen, I'm glad you did Peg...Aint half good to hear your voice after all these years.'
'Really? Well, that is a relief to hear. I often think of you, well us. Wondered where you'd be, who with, all the usual. So, how are you doing?'
Terry took a hefty sip of his Merlot.
'I'm not too bad as it happens, getting old like all of us, no real complaints though. You married Peg?'
'Was. Divorced. Few years ago. Jarry bloke, flash, mouthy. Bit of a berk really when I come to think of it. Got a kid by him. A girl called Stacey, a good kid…How about you Terry?'
Terry took another gulp of his red liquid.
'What married? No, no, never did. I've had a few birds over the years, but nothing ever stuck. Always seemed to end up in arguments. Washed my hands of all that palava, years ago now. Live a quiet life. Just me, my plants and my Daisy.'

'Did you say plants Terry Williams? Plants, haha?'
'Oi you, don't laugh. Yeh, I'm a gardener, or I was. Southwark Council parks team. My probation officer got me on that, when, you know... I'm retired now, did just over 30 years. I've got plants all over the flat I'll have you know. Some of them are my best mates.'
Peggy laughed at the last comment.

'And Daisy?'
'My dog. A flaming nuisance at times, but I love her really. Just don't tell her I said that.'
'You. A flipping gardener? Didn't expect that.'
'It was the stir Peg. It changed me. Almost the minute I was in there, I knew what a berk I'd been. I came out a different bloke. Not the one who, well, let you down...'

'Don't be silly, you never let me down. Listen, you fancy going out one evening?'
Terry quickly drained the remaining red wine in his glass, in one go.
'Sorry, I blurted that out a bit too quick...told you I was flaming nervous.'
'Eh? Well, not sure. Thing is Peg; it has been a long time aint it? All bit of a bolt out of the blue this. Can I have a think about it? That be alright?'
Peggy couldn't help but feel a little crestfallen. The call wasn't going the way she had hoped. However, she was determined to keep the conversation going.
'Oh, ok. I understand. Silly of me to think otherwise after this long really. I know its a shock me turning up like this, only, I've got something I really need to tell you.'
The large glass of red wine he had just drunk, caused Terry to drop his guard ever so slightly
'Oh yeh? What like?'
'Well, erm, it's not so easy to say on the phone.'
'Peg don't stop now. Tell me, please'
'Remember I mentioned my daughter Stacey earlier?
'Yeh…'
'Well. Actually, she's ours…'
Suddenly, Terry's mind went completely blank as he tried to take in what he had just been told.
'Ours? What do you mean ours? I mean, how come, I mean.

Are you saying that you were…?
Peggy suddenly felt a surge of energy and much more confident than she did when she first picked up the phone. By finally telling Terry the truth, it felt like a ton weight had been lifted off of her.
'Yeh, when you went away, I was pregnant.'
Terry's mind was now going round and round like a whirlpool, as he tried to think of dates and times and places from all those years ago.
'Peg, you… never... said...anything.'
'Yeh, I know. And I regret that now, but Terry it was hopeless. You had just gone down for fifteen and I find out, I'm having your kid. I was horribly lost. My mum went potty when I told her. She told me, I had to get away. In truth, I couldn't see what else I could do. So, we all got a transfer down to Croydon. Not long after that, I met my husband, and well, I took that route out of it. We married within a couple of months of meeting. Terry? You still there?'

Terry had poured himself another large measure of wine as he listened to Peggy.
'I don't know what to say Peg. I can't take it in. I need time to think.
Peggy nodded.
'Of course, I understand. Only thing is, time is a bit of a problem.'
Terry was now genuinely puzzled.
'What? Why?'
'Stacey's in a right state Terry. I'm losing her, she's on drugs and I'm at my wits end...'
Terry could hear the despair and dread in Peggy's voice.
'I'm genuinely sorry to hear that Peg, truly I am. But listen, I need time to think. Just dropping all this on me...I'm gonna need some time.'

‘Terry, I know. Trust me, I’ve thought long and hard for weeks before calling. Three times before tonight, I’ve gone to call you and three times I bottled out. I can only imagine what’s going on in your mind right now, but I need help. She needs help...’
‘Peggy, Peggy. Please love, I’ve gone blank here mate. I mean, it is great to hear from you, honest it is, but this, news... I just need…Look, give me your number and I’ll get back to you. I promise you I will.’

‘Oh Terry, but you might not, and I ...’
‘Listen Peg, I wouldn’t do that to you, you know that. Give you my word. I will call you back, I just need to have a think. Come on, give me your number...’
Terry carefully wrote it down on the back of an Evening Standard, that was laying nearby. He then said his goodbyes to Peggy and ended the call. He slowly put the phone on the arm of his armchair and reached for the half-finished bottle of Merlot and topped up his wine glass.

He took a decent sip of the drink and then his face broke out into a very big soppy grin.

7.
HELLO MORPHEUS, MY OLD FRIEND

A half bottle of red wine stood on a bedside cabinet, next to another empty bottle which now laid on its side near a three-quarter filled, drip stained, wine glass. Lying tangled up in his bed clothes Terry's mind raced with distant memories of Peggy, of when she was young and so beautiful. The smell of her hair and her favourite perfume was as strong in his nostrils as if it were from yesterday, instead of 40 years ago. His brain overloaded trying to work out years and months, to find out if it was possible, that he was the father to her daughter. As all this whirled around his already unsettled and now very pissed mind, he suddenly broke free from the recurring mania and came up for air, escaping the half dreams and long forgotten realities of his fractured attempts to sleep.

He sat up quickly, too quickly, and he had to grip his sheets, as the room quickly spun all around. He focused on Daisy asleep at the end of his bed and slowly the spinning stopped. He sat still on the edge of the bed, waiting for it to come to a complete stop. He then looked around him and then drained some more of the contents of the wine glass that was within his arms reach. He then drunkenly searched for his mobile phone and the copy of the Evening Standard upon which he wrote Peggy's number, both of which have been laying by his side on the bed all night.

Although, unable to find his glasses, he tried to enter his pin number, but kept hitting the wrong combination. Suddenly his eyes focussed enough for him to notice the time on the phone.

It was then he realised it was only 4am. He slowly released his grip on the device as his eyes drooped and soon, he was asleep. Dreaming he was looking for a toilet, he found a door with a number 1 painted on it. He opened the door and went in, only to find another door with a number 1 on it, then another, then another, then another. Going into that one finally revealed a urinal. He was about take a piss, when suddenly woke up in a shocked state. He frantically looked around and realised he was still in his bed. An embarrasing situation, narrowly avoided, he instead got up and stumbled to the bathroom.

Finished, he returned to his bed, and sat with his back against the headboard and reached for his phone. Having found his glasses in the chest pocket of his shirt, he put them on, and he tapped in his pin number. Within a few seconds the phone kicked into life and he saw he had missed calls from Peggy. It was now 6.30am.

Sensing movement, Daisy rose up from her sleeping position, doing a big stretch as she did so. She walked over towards Terry and licked the hand that was holding his phone. Terry smiled as he gently rubbed her head.

'Morning mate. Time for a pot of coffee I think and then I'll take you for a nice walk.'

Hearing the word walk, Daisy's ears pricked up and she rolled over on her back, beckoning Terry to rub her belly.

'Oh, it's time for the belly rub club is it? Ok then and then I've got a call to make.'

8.
IF A BURGER BE THE FOOD OF LOVE

A man with a Mediterranean complexion, wearing a small red and white paper hat, flipped a couple of beef burgers on a metal grill area behind a counter. He then scooped a couple of piles of chips onto white plates, edged in red and added the now cooked burgers to the slightly toasted buns already in position. He then hit a nearby bell. A smallish waiter, also in a red and white hat, picked up each plate and carried them to a nearby formica table, where Terry and Peggy are sat.

At that precise moment, they were the only ones in the restaurant. Terry was in a suit, complete with shirt and tie and Peggy in a nice floral dress. Terry watched the plates arrive at their table and acknowledged the waiter.
'Thanks mate.'
There was then an awkward silence as Peggy and Terry smiled at each other and then looked at the food in front of them.
'Well, tuck in then Peg.'
They both began to eat, whilst continuing to smile at each other between mouthfuls. Terry was quickly halfway through his meal, and he then stopped and rested his knife and fork on the edge of his plate.
'You look lovely Peg, if I may say so …'
Peggy's face reddened slightly
'Thank you, kind sir. You scrubbed up alright yourself mate.'
Terry laughed as he straightened his tie. He then ran his right index finger around the inside his shirt collar.
'Not worn one of those in years. Strangling me to be honest.'
Peggy let out a little laugh and it broke the tension between

them.
‘Glad you called Peg. Straight up.’
‘And I’m bloody glad you called back. Wasn’t sure you were going to.’
Terry smiled at her.
‘I said I would, didn’t I? Took some minerals though, if I’m honest.’
Peggy looks a little concerned.
‘Don’t look like that Peg. What I meant was, it was a bit of a shock hearing from you and well, you know, the news of the kid. A lot to take in one go that. ‘
Peggy looked at the tabletop and then at her food, which she had barely touched.
Terry puffed out his cheeks.
‘Blimey this is all very odd. I’ve not been out with a woman on my own, in years.’
‘Same. Not since my husband, y’know...’
A serious look come over Terry’s face and he looked at Peggy directly in the eyes. This unnerved her, as she failed to hold his gaze.
‘One question I got to ask Peg.’
Peggy looked at him with a serious expression etched all over her face.
‘Go on...’
‘What the flaming hell we doing in a Wimpy Bar? I mean, I remember you always liked a Brown Derby, but...come on girl…haha!’
Peggy quickly got a fit of the giggles.
‘Oooh you sod! I flaming panicked then!
And why here? Cos when you called, and asked where to meet, I could only think of one place, The Wimpy!’
A wistful look cames over Peggy’s face.
‘If truth be told, I don’t know anywhere else. I’m a bit lost really. How does that happen Terry? I feel like I’ve fallen

through the cracks...'
'You're not on your own love. Thousands and thousands of people in the same boat. Mad innit. Millions of people live in this country and so many are on their own. My Darren thinks I'm lonely, but I tell him I'm alone, but not lonely...'
Peggy looked sad.
'I am. Lonely, I mean...'
'Are ya Peg? Really. Got no mates?'
'Well, a couple, but most have moved away or died. Most nights, its bingo down the road and back home and early to bed. I'm not that old, not really, but I'm becoming old...'
'Aint we all girl. Sometimes it feels like our day is done and we're not really relevant anymore.'

Peggy took a very deep breath
'So, Stacey, our daughter…'
Terry instantly looked agitated and very uncomfortable.
'Don't know about you Peg, but I could suddenly do with a pint...'
He calls the waiter over.
'We're all done here cocker, very nice. What do I owe ya?'
The waiter looked concerned upon seeing their plates, which were still full of food.
'Everything is ok with the food?'
Terry stood up and put on his rainmac.
'It was 'andsome mate, honestly, but we're both full up. Look here's a score, that cover it?'
The waiter took the money and nodded.
'Lovely. Come on Peg, lets find a pub, we need a proper talk.'

Within ten minutes, Peggy is sat at a small round wooden pub table held up on iron legs, looking round at the other drinkers. Among the young couples that she guessed were out on first dates, she also noticed groups of men and women, all standing

around a larger table, which she imagined was an office after work drink.
Terry, tie now loosened, came back from the bar with a large white wine and a pint of lager and placed them on the table.
'Right then. To life.'
They touched glasses.
Terry then took a big gulp of the lager.
'Blimey, needed that. I mean I like a burger with the best of em, but...
Peggy took a sip of her wine and laughed.
'Behave you. What was I thinking?'
'Only playing. It's great seeing you Peg. Honestly mate'
'You too Terry. Been too long aint it. 40 years. A lifetime.'
Terry took another hit of his lager.
'As long as that Peg? Only kids, weren't we?
Peggy nodded.
'I was just a silly kid. A child really. '
Terry smiled at her.
'We both were. I know I wasn't grown up. Not really, mature like. Nowhere near it. Got a proper lesson on that inside.'
Peggy looked at him and suddenly saw the Terry she knew from all that time ago.
'I never really had the chance to ask why Terry?'
'Why? Why the robbery you mean?'
'Yeh, I never really saw you as any of that.'
'Truth is Peg. I wasn't. I knew that, the minute I was driving that getaway car. I was shitting myself. Totally out of my depth. I decided to quit there and then, but once in, really, they've got you. Trust me to get put away for a job I didn't do. It would be laughable, if I hadn't lost 10 years of my life.'
Peggy puts her hand on his.
'I remember you saying that in your letters. My mum said, 'They all say they didn't do it.'
Terry smiled at her.

‘She was funny your mum. Never liked me. Truth is, no one believed me, not even my mum. As for the one job I did do; well, it was simple really. I wanted nice things. I wanted to give you nice things. Only, when I was banged up, I then realised, I already had nice things...’
Peggy looks at him kindly, smiling.
Terry smiled back.
‘Too late then, of course...’

Peggy let go of Terry’s hands and took a good swig of her wine.
‘Looked like you needed that.’
Peggy winked at him.
Terry knew it was time to take the initiative.
‘So, Peg, tell me about Stacey.’
Her eyes immediately began to fill with tears. Terry now placed his right hand on hers, trying to reassure her.
‘Here now, that’s enough of that.’
‘I’m so sorry I didn’t tell you about her before. I thought about it a hundred times...’
Terry’s lips break out into a faint smile.
‘Never crossed my mind, I had a kid Peg. Not once.
‘I heard you had got out; word had reached me down in Croydon. Stacey was coming up to 11 then and I wanted then to tell you, but I couldn’t. My old man, Derek, always thought she was his. So, I let him. Easier that way.’
Terry looked off into the mid distance, picking up his pint.
‘What might have been eh?’
‘She’s in such a mess now Terry, involved with terrible people. I know, deep down, she’s a good person really, but my God she’s landed herself in a mess.‘
‘Drugs you said.’
‘Yeh, all sorts. Proper street junkie’
Terry bowed his head.

‘Horrible word that.’

‘She was as good as gold as a kid, did well at school, really bright. But then she got heavily into going out. Nightclubs, warehouse parties, them raves... She just drifted away from me. I’d find myself driving round at 4am trying to find her and then when I did, she’d be out of her head. Derek was fucking hopeless. Stace and him clashed badly anyway. They never got on, so in the end, he washed his hands of her. She left home at 18. Occasionally she’d drift back home, but only for money really and when that ran out, I’d find things missing around the house. She was robbing me blind. Me, her own mum. Then, gradually, she stopped coming back all together and then the phone calls stopped.
Terry was playing with his pint glass, rolling it one side to the other on the pub table.
‘Once they get on that gear that badly, they’ve only one aim each day and that’s to earn enough, to get more. Normal rules do not apply. You not seen her for a bit then?’
‘No, I’ve seen her recently. She’s basically on the streets. She’s lost in a world of drink and drugs Terry. A fucking horrible world. She hangs out near here actually, in Kennington Park. There’s a big group of ‘em. I’ve watched her, well out of sight of course. It was being back here, and doing that, that I thought of you.’

Terry suddenly sat up straight.
‘Round here? There’s a little firm up by the table tennis tables, by the old water fountain in the park?’
Peggy nodded.
‘Sounds like them.’
‘Seen ‘em when I’m out with Daisy. They play junkie ping pong. Proper state. Got to be the same crowd. 30 handed or so most days. How did you find her there?

Peggy dropped her head and sighed.
'I had some court papers come to my house. There was a fine to pay, couple of hundred quid. I guessed she'd given them my address when they nicked her. It was for shop lifting and pick pocketing, with the offence taking place in Selfridges, but she was picked up for it in SE11. I had to smile when I saw that. She was back from where I was from. Like a flipping homing pigeon or something. So, I drove down here and toured around and a couple of days later, I saw that group you know of, and there she was.'

Peggy then slid a photograph over to Terry's side of the table. He smiled at it.
'That's her, around the last time I was seeing her regularly.'
Terry couldn't stop smiling.
'Pretty kid.'
'She was yeh, and she always reminded me of you. Not only in looks, but nature as well.'
Terry couldn't help but notice the resemblance to him in his younger days, staring back at him in the photo on the pub table.
'You know, Daisy growls at that lot when we're down there. She's not having any of 'em. Clouds of that horrible skunk as you walk past. Stinks to high heaven that shit.'
Peggy was now looking very serious.
'I'm worried Terry. She's getting too old for that life; her health won't hold out much longer on all that crap she's taking. Crack, weed, the drink, and God knows what else. I guess the hoisting and dipping was to pay for her gear off the main fella in her mob. I overheard someone call him Task the other day. Looks a right wrong 'un. Anyway, he's got some hold over her. Look, I'm frightened to even ask you this, but would you try and speak to her, now you know?

Terry looked confused.

‘Do what Peg? Me? I don’t know about that. I mean, why would she listen to me, a complete stranger, even if I could get near her?’
Peggy nodded at him.
‘I know, I know. Seems mad to even ask, but I’m at my wits end and desperate Tel. I doubt she’ll last much longer out there living like that. And, well... she is your….’

Terry never heard Peggy say the word daughter. His mind was now full of thoughts of how do I get out of this, I mean I don’t even know if she is really mine?
‘Listen Peg, I’m getting on mate, I’m past it. Looking for a quiet life.’
Terry couldn’t help but notice the look of sadness that came over Peggy’s face as he spoke. He then felt terrible for doubting that Stacey was his kid. The photo he had just seen was strong enough evidence really and he knew that. He sat there weighing up his options, when in reality, he knew if Stacey was really his daughter, then he had no options.
‘Tell you what Peg, I’ll wander down there and have a look eh?’
Peggy smiled at him, knowing that was probaly the best she was going to get from him that evening.
‘Thanks Terry, that means so much to me. How about one for the road? I’ll get ‘em. Same again?’
Terry nodded.
‘Why not. Lovely. We’ll raise a toast to Stacey.’
Whilst Peggy was at the bar, he frantically tried to take in all that was going on and he puffed out his cheeks as he contemplated what is to come.
‘Fuck me’ he said to himself quietly ‘I thought my superhero days were well and truly over.’

A young couple on an adjoining table, looked Terry’s way

after hearing him speak to himself. The woman whispered to her bloke.
'What did he just say?'
The fella looked at Terry with pity in his eyes.
'Something about him being Superman or something. Geezers mullered.'
Terry heard them both and couldn't help but smile to himself as he looked straight ahead.

'You two wait till you see me in my cape…'

9.
WASTERS

The hood of Terry's puffa coat was pulled up tight, in an attempt to keep out a fresh wind as he sat on a pub bench, outside The Rose, a pub close to Kennington Park. He had a pint of lager in front of him, which he had hardly touched. It was now coming up to 5pm and his current view was one of hundreds of pairs of commuter legs walking past him, with the majority heading towards the nearby Oval tube station, though some hopped on buses. Daisy occasionally barked at groups of school kids in black uniforms, who walked around being as loud as possible. Most stuffing their faces with chicken shop chips smothered in red sauce, in between the shouting.

Despite all these distractions going on around him, Terry's focus remained on one man. He was the central figure standing in the middle of a scruffy, dirty, ramshackle, mob of around 30 people of all ages and colours, standing within the park, just a few hundred yards away. From observing him, Terry was now sure this was the one Peggy called Task in the pub. Terry saw that every transaction, had to receive a nod of approval from this fella first. He was the puppet master pulling the strings of his own group of odd-looking puppets. Suddenly, Terry saw a rake thin shape of a man, walking with a metal crutch, dressed all in black, including the crocs on his feet, walk up and speak to Task. They talked into each others ear and then shook hands. The thin man then nodded, as he put his hand in his right trouser pocket and left the park, by a side gate, not far from Terry's bench. Terry was up quickly and soon heading for the same exit.
'Come on Daisy girl, lively mate, his leg must be getting better'

As casually as he could make it appear, Terry then bumped into the same thin man as he emerged onto the Kennington pavement.
'Sorry mate, I didn't …Oh, alright Brian, apologies pal, lost my footing there, flipping dog nearly had me over?'
Brian looked genuinely shocked to have run into Terry
'Oh, alright Tel, mate? All good with you? Listen, sorry, I can't stop, I'm…'
As Brian then tried to step around Terry, Terry blocked any thought of a quick getaway.
'Blimey, that's a result, bumping into you like this.'
Brian tried once again to get by him.
'Hold tight Brian, where ya going mate? Didn't you hear me. I need a word.'
Brian sensed he would now struggle to get away easily and so gave in trying.
'Want a word? With me? What for? What's up?'
Terry affected a confused look on his face.
'Up? Nothings up?'
Brian moved slightly to his right.
'Well, what you stopping me for like?
'I just want a word that's all. Chrissakes, stand still a minute, will ya! What are you bouncing about for?'
Terry now had hold of Brian's right arm. Brian looked down at the grip, and then back to Terry
'Tel, mate, I can't dwell, telling ya, got a lot on…'
Terry took a firmer grip of the arm.
'Did you hear about your neighbour?'
Brian looked puzzled.
'Neighbour? What one? Tel, I aint got a clue what you are on about?'
Terry looked at Brian with utter contempt and Brian finally stopped bouncing.
'Dolly Brian, Dolly.'

Brian grinned.
'Oh that, yeah. As it happens, I heard someone down the pub say he had a kicking or something. Par for the course for that lot, though aint it?
Terry looked Brian square in the eyes.
'That lot Brian, what d'ya mean?'
Brian suddenly began to feel nervous. He didn't like the way this conversation was going,
'Well, you know, the lavenders…The gays mate. Anyway, got fuck all to do with me. Tel, listen I gotta chip mate.'
'Yeh, in a minute. Just want a word first. Only…bit delicate like.'
Brian looked Terry up and down, still in a very confused state.

'Ummm see, I'm looking for a bag of weed Brian.'
Brian did a double take look at at Terry.
'What?'
'Just a bit you know. Medicinal reasons. I'm full of aches and pain's in my back, and my mate told me that a puff of that of a night, would help. He was after some too as it happens, but for more recreational reasons in his case.
Brian continued to look at Terry quizzically.
'Right, right. So, what you asking me for?'
'Well, I was speaking to Del about it the other day and he mentioned you. Said you got a few deals going on.'
'Did he for fucks sake…Fucking Del...Trappy mug.'
Terry tried hard to suppress a smile.
'I know, fucking people eh? But is it true? Could you sort me some?'
Brian studied Terry, trying to work out if this is a wind up or not.
'You being straight here Terry? Like, this aint a gee up is it'
'Gee up Brian? I'm in agony here son.'
Brian nodded.

‘Well. I might be able to help. Depends on how much you want. I’ve got regulars already waiting, and in the queue well before you, you get me?’

Terry kissed his lips together.
‘Yeh, I get you. But well, that’s a bit tricky that, cos I want it as fast as possible. Not feeling well enough to wait.‘
‘I aint Sainsbury’s Terry. You don’t just walk up my aisle and pick up what you need mate.’
Terry looked at Brian in near astonishment at that picture Brian had just conjured up.
‘Quite, quite, no I get that, I do. Only, can’t you introduce me to who you get it from?’
Brian smiled and looked at Terry, as if he was mad.
‘Oh, do fuck off. Are you mad?’
Terry smiled.
‘Do you know where I’m on the way to now Brian?
Brian shook his head and smiled at Terry.
‘Not really my concern is it Tel? Getting your pension? How the fuck would I know?’

Terry grinned an even wider grin.
‘Get my pension, like it. No, I’m off to talk to the old bill.’
Brian suddenly stopped smiling. He beckoned Terry down into an alleyway between two shops and propped his crutch up against a wall.
‘Old bill? What you want with them?’
Terry leaned in a bit closer to Brian and dropped his voice virtually to a whisper.
‘Well, I said to Dolly, I’d heard him rowing with someone the other night, and that maybe, whoever he was rowing with, might have then given him the slap in the street. Dolly nodded and said maybe I should report what I heard to the plod.‘
Brian licked his lips, his mouth drying out by the second.

'And did Dolly happen to mention who he was rowing with?' Terry was now so close to Brian, he could smell the fear, among other unpleasant aromas coming off him.
'Yeah, he did. I said to Dolly, listen, I want a quiet life, no dramas, so didn't really want to get involved. But you know, he's a mate, so maybe I should tell what I heard.'

Brian tried his best to smile over gritted teeth.
'Ok, ok. No need to get the filth busy is there?
Maybe I could get you a meet with my fella, you might then forget the conversation with Dolly?'
Terry leaned back from Brian, the heady mixture of body odour and skunk, now beginning to make him feel nauseous.
'Yeh, well if you could, I'll swerve the coppers. Tell you what, do that and I'll stick a nice drink on top just for you as well. Hows that sound?'
Brian looked at Terry very warily, but knew he had little option. He looked up and down the alleyway, desperate to get away.
'Alright, I'll do it, but it'll take me a couple of calls to sort. If all goes alright, meet me at that gate over there, tomorrow afternoon 2ish. I'll slip a note under your door later confirming all that and I'll give you the price for a quarter. You'll get enough to smoke out of that, for you and your mate, if you go half each.
Terry made a mental note of the park entrance that Brian nodded to.
'Sweet.'
'No fucking about though Terry. These aint nice people I'm dealing with. Get me? Pure business.'
Terry nodded.
'Ok Brian, nothing silly from me.'
With that Terry walked away from Brian slowly, looking down towards his dog.
'Come on Daisy girl, lets get you home. There's

a lot of rubbish out on the street tonight…'

10.
A ROUTINE MATTER

A beautiful bright early morning welcomed Terry as he stepped out of the main front door of his block, and onto its surrounding streets. Daisy, as ever, was by his side, her brown leather lead, fastened to the handle of the tartan trolley that Terry was pushing. It was Saturday morning and as regular as clockwork, he had his routine to follow. First stop as usual was Guray's. Terry peered through the steamed-up shop window as he arrived and smiled as he watched the baker pulling hot bread out of an even hotter oven.

The freshly baked smell then hit Terry right in the nostrils as he walked in. The two men were soon in an animated conversation as Guray wrapped up the individual elements of Terry's order into different sized, plain white paper bags. Terry then packed these away carefully in his shopping trolley. He bid his Turkish friend goodbye and headed to Amin's to collect his newpaper order. Once that was all safely gathered in, Daisy led Terry to a bench on the grassy area of the estate, and they each had a breather watching the world go by, before heading back to their block.

The order of the dropping off the goods, never changed. Elsie first and she was waiting by her front door as Terry hit her landing for the hand over. Dolly next and despite his recent troubles, he put on a brave face and very quickly he and Terry were laughing. However, that abruptly stopped, as once again Dolly knocked Terry back, and avoided paying his bill.

Finally, Gloria, rock steady and solid Gloria, who in the conversation that followed between them, ended up checking

up as much on Terry, as he did on her. Once finished, Terry made his way back to his own flat, deadheading fading flowers in his hanging baskets as he did so. Noticing the earth was on the dry side, he unclipped Daisy from her lead, leaving her to wander up and down their landing, whilst he made his way indoors. There, he filled his green plastic watering can, before returning to give his beloved plants a good soak. For the next half hour or so, he was lost in the green world of his balcony and only the whining of a hungry dog, broke that spell.
'Breakfast time is it?'
Daisy cocked her head to one side at the mention of the word breakfast. Terry smiled at her.
'Thought it might be.'

A few hours later, Darren was trying to get into Terry's block, but got no answer from his uncle to let him in. Instead, he called Gloria and she kindly buzzed him in. Once on the landing, he pressed Terry's doorbell. He waited for the usual noises from inside, only there was only silence and no sign of life. Darren tried the bell again and once again, there was no response. He lifted up the silver-coloured metal flap of Terry's letterbox and peered through.
'Unc! Terry! You in there?'
He continued to look through into the very quiet flat, even though there was no response.
'Bollocks. Where's he gone? TERRY! Oh, for fucks sake.'

Gloria came out of her flat to investigate.
'No sign of him? How odd?'
Gloria then thoughtfully rubbed her chin.
'You know, I heard his door go earlier, and thought that was a little funny.'
Darren was getting more than a little concerned
'Funny? In what way Mrs Dyer?'

‘Well, I popped out when I heard his door shut and then looked over the balcony and noticed him leaving the estate. Only, he had no Daisy with him. So very rare to see him without her. I can only guess he left her with Elsie?’
Darren looked puzzled.
‘Yeh, that is odd? Didn’t say a word to me and I’ve just checked the diary on my phone, and we were definitely due a catch up today.’

Darren glanced at his watch, and then over the red bricked balcony, to double check, but there was no sign of his uncle.
‘I’ll have to call him.’
Just as he finished that sentence, his mobile phone suddenly rang.
Darren looked at the phone, and he saw Terry’s name appear as the caller. Darren smiled.

‘Where are you? Everything alright? Yeh, I’ve been here ten minutes. Eh? Terry, why are you whispering? You’re where? Why there? Eh? Hang on, you’re breaking up, Terry…Ok, what end you at? Table tennis tables, yeh I know it. Stay there, be with you in 15 minutes.’
Terry’s voice suddenly became much louder.
Darren grimaced though as he struggled to hear his uncle.
‘Eh? No, sorry, didn’t catch that, breaking up mate.’
Once again, Terry’s loud voice booms from within the phone.
‘Nope, no good. Lost ya. I’ll see you in 15….’
Darren ended the call and put the phone in his right trouser pocket and began to head for the lift.
‘He’s over the park. God knows why? I’ll go and find him. See you later Mrs Dyer.’
Gloria smiled at him as he entered the lift.
‘Gloria. Call me Gloria, please…’

11.
PARKLIFE

Over by Kennington park, Terry put his phone in his trouser pocket.
'Bollocks.'
Truth be told, he was more than a little edgy as he carefully scanned the people all around him, looking for any sign of Brian.
Terry glanced at his watch. It was 2pm on the dot. Suddenly, he received a tap on his shoulder, which made him jump.
'Jesus! Fuck me, Brian…'
'Alright Tel. Bit nervous aintcha?'
Brian smiled a gap-toothed smile at him.
'Me? Nah, you surprised me, thats all.'
'Yeh whatever mate. Got me note then? Trust you've got the wedge?
Terry looked directly at the waster now in front of him and nodded, patting his left trouser pocket as he did so.
'My mate said 150 nicker was well over the asking rate by the way.'
Brian shook his head.
'Fuck me, what are you like. You wanted a rush job, which trust me, wasn't easy to sort, and still, you moan at the price. Don't forget, my fee is part of that and you're buying a good grade here, not the normal floor sweepings served up on our estate. So, do me a favour, shut the fuck up Terry.'
'Alight, alright. Just saying Brian.'
'Give it here then...'
'Eh? What?'
'What do you mean what?' The dough Tel. That's the only way it's going to work today. The geezer don't know you, but he does me. Me, he'll deal with me, you, he won't. So, gis it

here.'
Terry reluctantly handed over the envelope.

Brian started to open the evelope. Terry stopped him
'It's all there trust me. No need to count it.'
Brian looked at Terry and smiled.
'Better be.'
He then nodded and turned his back to the street and now faced the green and brown hedge that surrounded the park and walked towards the nearest entry gate, his crutch tapping out a decent rhythm as he did so. Terry followed, close behind.
'Spoke to Del this morning. Reckoned he never told you about me being able to serve you up?'
Terry smiled at him.
'Did he? Well, we both know he's a born liar. How else would a silly old fucker like me know where to go?'
Terry casually looked away down the street.
Brian looked unconvinced.
'Well, spose so. Anyway, we're here now so come on, time to crack on. Don't want to be late.'
Brian quickened the pace up to 'junkie trot', his metal walking aid, not touching the floor. Terry found himself struggling to keep up. As they entered the park, Terry sensed Brian beginning to tense up. They were now only 50 foot away from the large group gathered together, up ahead.

The scene Terry looked upon was an odd one. Old traditional park bench drinkers, mixed with street junkies, mixed with youths dressed in all black, their faces partly covered with masks of the same colour. A couple of them were eating slices of pizza straight out of the cardboard takeaway boxes they had arived in, whilst perched on a 'free to play' table tennis table. The rubbish bins near them were overflowing with empty fast-food boxes. Various tins and bottles of lager were all around

their feet. Clouds of sickly smelling bluish - grey smoke rose above their heads.
They were loud, boisterous and at the necessary times, threatening to the normal passers-by, be it a bloke walking his dog, or a mum with a baby in a pram, who had strayed a little too close to them.
A fella in a wheelchair, with half his right leg missing, was cradling a boom box, which blared out old school hip hop and three others were sitting astride green and white hire bikes. Two large XL bully type dogs roamed in and around looking for any scraps of food. Two men were playing table tennis on an adjoining nearby table that the council had provided. Terry couldn't help but notice that despite one of them wearing white cricket pads and both of them appearing to be pissed as puddings, they played a decent standard of ping pong.

Brian looked around nervously, scanning for the main man. The general noisy chatter among the mob, slowly became quieter, as their attention became focused on Brian and Terry. A tall, light skinned fella in his mid to late 40s, held court on a nearby park bench. Sensing it having gone quiet, he had stood up to have a look round. Terry sussed this was the man he saw talking to Brian the day before. This was Task.
'Oi, oi, you lot, shut up will ya. Cut the tunes. I want eyes and ears on these two, hear me?'
His accent was one of pure street South East London.
A couple of the younger ones, late teens, early 20s, broke off from the main group and stood either side of Brian and Terry.

Task slowly moved towards him and Brian. Terry noticed Task had a busted left leg, that didn't seem to bend, resulting in a very pronounced limp. He wore a light grey jogging bottoms and sweatshirt combination, set off by a pair of gleaming white Nike trainers. Blue and black tattoos emerged from the top of the sweatshirt and rose up his neck and both of his hands were covered in ink..

Brian held out his fist.
'Alright Task? This is Terry, the geezer I mentioned.'
Task looked at Brian's fist, but left it hanging and then looked Terry up and down, smiling and sneering in equal measure.
'What you doing here old man?'
Terry looked a little confused and glanced at Brian.
'I, er, I thought Brian…'
Task put his right index finger to his lips and then he spoke slowly, almost in a whisper.
'Sssshhh old man, ssshhh. Brian has told me what you are after. My question though was, what you doing here? I mean there's loads of places you could do a little puff deal. What brings you to my ends?'
Terry knew he was being tested.
'As I told Brian, I mentioned to a mate of mine, well ours, that I've got a fucked back and he said a bit of a puff might relieve the pain. I said where do I go for that and he put Brian's name in the frame.'
Task looked at Brian.
'That right?'
Brian struggled to look at Task but nodded somewhat reluctantly. Task looked back towards Terry.
'Well, I'm no doctor, but yeh, I've heard it helps. Discussed the price with you has he?
Terry nodded towards Brian.
'Yeh, and he's holding my wedge.'
Task gestured for Brian to hand it over.
Terry slowly looked round and noticed everyone was now staring at him. A young white kid dressed head to toe in black, looking no more than 16 noticed Terry looking at him. Withouth breaking his return gaze at Terry, he casually spat on

the gravel path, narrowly missing Terry's Reebok's. He then sarcastically smiled at Terry, who though he was bursting inside wanting to grab the kid and batter him, simply smiled back. He then continued to scan the crowd scene and then stopped and looked carefully at a blonde woman. He squinted as he tried to focus on her features. She had tired looking baggy eyes, set into an under weight, lined face. He also noticed she had a front tooth missing and her grubby, old looking hands, had DIY tattoos on them. He thought he read 'Stacey' in patchy blue ink, on the back of her right hand, as she lifted it for a drag on her cigarette. In her left, she carried a large yellow paper Selfridges bag. She looked unsteady on her feet and a little pissed.

'Know you, don't I love?'
Terry had decided to take a punt.
The blonde woman looked at him with confusion and utter contempt.
'What's he say? He talking to me?
Terry pressed on.
'Yeh, I know you from somewhere?'
Stacey laughed at him.
'Fuck off do ya... Fucking senile mate.'
The mob smiled and laughed at Terry, who simply smiled back.
'Nah, no I do.'
Stacey was now looking at Terry very suspicously through her red blotchy eyes.
'Sharon? Stella? Something like that.'
'Stacey mate, her name's Stacey…'
The blonde woman quickly turned round and glared at the dopey looking unfortunate who had shouted out her name. She then walked up and hit him as hard as she could in his stomach. Dopey fell to his knees, gasping for breath.
'Shut. Your. Fucking. Gob!'

After waiting for the laughter to die down, Terry struck.
'Stacey! That's' it!'

'Task, who the fuck is this geezer? Seriously jarring my nerves mate.'
Task was now looking at Stacey.
'Not sure Stace? Here to do a deal but seems more interested in you. You sure he's not an old regular, come back to revisit old times?'
Stacey carefully looked Terry up and down.
'Nah, don't know him. Swear to ya.'

Task now turned and glared at Terry.
'Well, he seems to know you girl.'
Terry felt the pressure building and realised, it was shit or bust time.
'Stacey, it was your mum who told me where to find you love.'
Stacey's eyes began to redden and tears formed.
'My mum? How'd you know my mum?'
'It's a very long story love, and one for another time. But now, we have to leave.. This mob are fucking wrong 'uns girl, the lot of 'em.'
Task was now staring hard at Brian.
'What the fuck have you brought me here Brian?'
Brian could feel the sweat on his top lip as he struggled to hold Task's gaze.
'I swear to you Task, all I know is he is a punter looking for some bud. Straight up mate. That's all I know,'
Brian's eyes wander over to Terry's face.

'Tel, what the fuck you doing?'
Terry's gaze never left Stacey.
'Shut up, you fucking lowlife mug.'
Brian looked back at Task and knew for sure; this wasn't going

to end well.
Terry began to walk towards Stacey.
'Come here girl, its time.'
Stacey was now frightened rigid and slowly backed away from him.
'Nah mate, nah, I ain't going nowhere with you. Don't know ya, ya nonce.'
Task looked at the 2 men that had slowly separated from the crowd. He then nodded towards Terry.
'Fucking hurt him. I want him hurt.'

Terry made a grab for Stacey, but as he did so, he was hit powerfully in his ribs. The blow felt like a sledgehammer had been let loose on him. He fell to his knees, gasping for air and franctically trying to catch a breath. Two hard punches then landed on the side of his head, and he fell face first onto the gravel path. His ears were now ringing, and everything suddenly sounded like it was under water. Thankfully, air slowly returned to his lungs and he gupled it in deeply. He struggled up onto his hands and knees. Globules of spit and snot dripped from his chin and nose and splattered on the ground beneath him.

Knowing he was in a bad place, Terry slowy turned his head and tried to focus on the figures looming in front of him. Before he could make out a face, a powerful kick landed in his rib area, directly on the other side from the first hit. He tried to cover up, but before he could do so, a fist hit him again in his right ear. He felt like he is about to lose consciousness. He frantically tried to open his eyes, but all was very blurry and out of focus. He wiped them with his right hand, and felt a wet, slightly sticky substance, which he knew was blood. He also knew he was done. All his energy had gone, and he collapsed and then rolled onto his back, and lay still. He opened his eyes and the blue sky and white fluffy clouds above, slowly came back into sharp focus. Hearing footsteps close by, he turned his head towards the noise and and saw Task stroll up to Brian and calmly head butt him. Brian fell to the path like a bag of cement, holding his head and face.

Even through the intense pain he was now suffering from, Terry couldn't help but smile a weak smile as he thought of how much Dolly would have loved to have seen that. Just as he was about to drift off into unconsciousness, he could sense a figure running fast towards him. Slowly, he tried to pull his knees up and roll up into a ball on his right-hand side, but he was too slow and instead recieved a hard, swift kick to his bollocks from a bright white pair of Stan Smiths. He let out a strangled groan as the searing pain shot up into his brain. Through all that, he became aware of someone shouting at him.

The sound was muffled and incoherent at first, but it slowly cleared to reveal it was Stacey screaming at him.

'Who the fuck are you, you fucking wrong 'un!?! Keep away, you hear me?

Come near me again, I'll shank ya, and that's a fucking promise,'

Terry kept his eyes closed, as he tried to shout with the little energy that he had left. Despite his best efforts, it came out as a faint whisper.

'I'm… your…dad love….'

He then blacked out.

He was now flat on his back, both arms outstretched either side of his body. Brian, blood trickling down from a very red nose, managed to get up onto his knees and then upright, by clinging onto his crutch. He took a quick look at Terry and then staggered towards an exit, stumbling past a small crowd

of onlookers, most of whom were now filming the scene in front of them, on their phones.
Task grabbed Stacey tightly by her arm and began dragging her out of the park, closely followed the rest of the mob, who then quickly dispersed in different directions.

Darren had arrived in the park, just in time to see his uncle roll over onto his back. He was now running as fast as he could towards Terry. He shoved through the crowd and sat down by Terry's unconscious, lifeless body, cradling his cut and bleeding head.
'It's alright unc. Its alright mate, I'm here…'
He pulled out his mobile phone and dialled 999.
'Hello… Ambulance, please… as quick as you can, I beg of you.'

12.
THE DOCTOR WILL SEE YOU NOW

All was very quiet in Terry's hospital room. A gentle breeze blew through the once white, now cream, paper blinds hanging by the main window. Terry was sound asleep, mainly due to the heavy pain relief drugs he had been prescribed. His face was battered and bruised and a good third of it now covered in bits of white dressing. Darren was sat on the only chair in the room and idly scrolled through his phone, when the patchy Wi -Fi signal allowed him to do so.

Suddenly, the door to the room swung open and a senior looking nurse entered, closely followed by young man in a longish white coat, under which a blue and white striped shirt, and blue and white polka dot bow tie, could be seen. The man in white looked at the paperwork, then at Terry and then at Darren
'Family?'
'Yeh, nephew. Darren.'
'Hello Darren. I'm Doctor Churcher and this is ward sister Nicholson.'
The sister looked at Darren, smiled and nodded gently.
'OK, right, well, your uncle will be ok, you'll be pleased to know. X-rays show a couple of cracked ribs, and of course he has plenty of cuts and lacerations to his face, plus severe inflammation to his, umm, shall we say, more tender parts. Apart from that, he's fine. He'll be in a lot of pain for a few days, the ribs playing him up mostly, but we'll dose him up with some happy pills. Will you or someone be around to keep an eye on him during the day and evening?'

‘Oh yeh, I’ll be around when I can, and he has some good neighbours who’ll pop in.’
The doctor smiled and then ticked a couple of boxes on the papers he was carrying.
‘Good, then he can go home this afternoon...’
Darren looked agahst.
‘Eh? This afternoon? Really? He looks terrible and...’
The doctor grinned at Darren, as he cut across him.
‘We’ve carefully monitored him overnight, and he was fully compos mentis this morning, with maybe just a slight hint of concussion. The need of that bed he is occupying is our main priortiy, which is always the case I’m afraid. Besides he’ll heal quicker at home with you looking after him...’

Darren looked at Terry and wasn’t sure what to say.
‘Right, right, but…’
The doctor handed his notes to the sister and he began to walk out of the room.
‘We’ll get the ward staff to organise transport home. I take it, you’ll be going with him?’
‘Yeh, sure. OK, I better start to get his things together.’
‘No rush, er…Darren wasn’t it? Yes, good, ummm these things can take a while.’
The sound of voices had stirred Terry. He slowly opened his eyes and the bright room lights, caused him to flinch as he did so. He reached up with his right hand to feel his face and his fingers patted the extensive dressing.
The doctor noticed Terry’s movements. He leant over and bent back the top of the paperwork, that the Sister was now carrying, looking for the first name of the man now waking up.
‘How are you feeling Mr Williams…ummm Terry, isnt it?
Terry nodded and then attempted to talk, but his throat was parched, and his lips dry. The sister poured some water from

a clear plastic jug, which sat on his bedside cabinet, into a stumpy plastic beaker and offered it to Terry.
'Just a couple of sips now, don't rush it.'
Terry smiled at her as she placed her right hand and forearm behind his head and raised him towards the drink. After a couple of small gulps, he coughed a little which brought more pain his way from his rib area.
'I'm ok Doc. Bit sore, but y'know...'
His voice was soft and low, sounding only on about half power.
'Good, good. Well, you took quite a bang. I was just saying to, er, Darren, you are now ready to go home, as you have told the sister, you aren't looking to press any charges...'
Darren quickly looked up at the doctor.
'No charges? Hang on. What do you mean no charges?'
Terry waved his right hand towards his nephew
'Darren, leave it. That's right Doc. It was a total misunderstanding that got out of hand, that's all.'
Darren looked at his uncle, with total confusion etched all over his face.
Doctor Churcher looked at Darren, but he had little or no desire to get involved any further.
'Your call of course Terry. I understand we've informed the local police of your decision and they are happy to leave it, if you are. They are already aware of the group from which some of your attackers came, so will continue to monitor them. Hopefully transport shouldn't be too long, and then when home, if you have any problems, you know where we are. Ok, Sister, all yours...Take care now Terry.'

The Doctor looked at Darren and nodded. He and the sister then left the room. Darren waited for a few seconds and then blew up.
'Terry, what the fuck is going on here?'
Terry shut his eyes and spoke very slowly.

‘Son, not now. All I want to do is get home and get in my own bed. I just want to go home mate.
Get me indoors son, all revealed there. Promise’

13.
CONFESSION

Terry gingerly walked into his front room and carefully sat himself down into his favourite battered, brown, leather armchair, wincing as he did so.
Darren, carrying a couple Tesco carrier bags full of Terry's clothing and toiletries, was only a couple of steps behind, ready to catch his uncle if needed. The effort of getting from the passsenger transport to where he was now sitting, had taken every ounce of the little energy Terry had left. He threw back his head and breathed in deeply trying to get some air into his tired and aching body. This rattled his ribs and reminded him to take it easy.

Once he was happy Terry was safe and secure in his chair, Darren walked to the kitchen and put the kettle on. He filled two white mugs with milk, and granulated coffee.
'I got Elsie's number off Mrs. Dyer, Daisy's fine. Kettles on.'
'What?'
Terry struggled to hear Darren above the rumbling kettle and the constant ringing in his ears.
'I said..., oh bollocks. Wait...'
Darren put a couple of teaspoons, the sugar bowl and a side plate full of bourbons onto a tray and then once in the front room, placed the tray on the house plant cluttered coffee table. He then repeated what he had just said about Elsie and Daisy.
'Oh good, ta boy. Remind me, I owe Else a Cinzano or three.'
Darren stayed in the front room with Terry, while waiting for the kettle to boil.
'She was full of questions, bless her. Told her, all revealed later.'
Terry leaned back into his chair; his eyes closed. He smiled at

the thought of Elsie not knowing what was going on.
'She won't like being in the dark, her. Does love a slice of gossip that woman.'
Darren heard the click of the now boiled kettle in the kitchen and got up to sort. He returned with two white mugs full of hot, steaming coffee. He placed them on the tray on Terry's coffee table, close to Terry's chair.
'Its me first though unc..."
Terry didn't open his eyes.
'I need to get my head down boy, can't it wait?'
Darren smiled.
'Noooo, come on, I need to know what the fuck is going on here.'
Terry exhaled and then opened his eyes, as he searched his mind, looking for where to start...

Meanwhile, ten miles away, a very worried looking Peggy walked around and around her front room. It had been two days since she had heard from Terry. She had called him five times on his mobile, but he hadn't picked up, or replied to her voicemails and she was now getting very anxious. Even though she hadn't smoked for coming up to three years, she was now leaving a trail of grey ash on her oatmeal carpet, as she puffed on a cigarette, from a half packet of fags she had found in a kitchen drawer. She hoped they would steady her nerves, but in reality, they were making her feel sick.

A list of possible scenarios constantly visited her mind, each one leaving her feeling more frightened and concerned than the previous one.
Suddenly, her telephone burst into life, causing her to jump. She quickly picked up the receiver and noticed it read private number.
"Terry that you...Tel..'

She was greeted by silence from the other end. Peggy tried again.
'Hello? Is there anyone there?'
'Mum? Mum, it's me...'
Peggy's face crumpled upon hearing her daughter's voice.
'Oh Stace...Stacey love…'
'Who is he mum? The big fella?
Peggy had a shocked look all over face, as she heard Stacey speak.
'What fella?'
'He said he knew you mum and you'd told him where to find me. Who was he mum? I need to know. Mum, I…NEED… TO…FUCKING…KNOW…'
Peggy was now trembling, and her hands were very clammy.
'You've seen him? Terry? Where' d 'you see him? Where love?'
'Aint got much time mum. I just need to know...'
Peggy began to sob quietly, as she weighed up what to say next.
'Can't we do this face-to-face love? Not that easy on the pho...'
Stacey had heard her mum crying and she too was now fighting back the tears.
A silence fell between them. Five seconds felt like five minutes.
'Mum, you still there? Please tell me…'
'He's... your dad... Stace...Terry. My very first love. He's your dad, Stace...'

Stacey held the phone receiver away from her ear and stared into middle distance.
Peggy could now hear nothing but an overwhelming silence.
'You still there love? Stacey? Come home. Can you hear me Stacey? Come home, begging you love...'
'But…what about Derek?'

Peggy smiled and wept at the same time.
'I told Derek you were his, but you weren't. I was pregnant with you when Terry went inside. He's your father. Derek was always useless with sums, and just never tumbled it. Or if he did, he never said anything to me.'
'Prison? Bad boy was he, Terry?'
'No not really. Long time ago. Just young and silly and in love with me. Wanted to give me the best, so he went robbing. I've only just told him about you love...'
Stacey smiled.
'Bet that was a shock for him. Why now mum?'
'Cos I need his help. You'll die out there soon. I know it and you know it. Either the drugs or the drink or that evil bastard you're wrapped around will KILL you. You need to stop; You know you do; I can feel you know that. It's only a matter of time. You need to come home...'

Tears slowly trickled from Stacey's blackened eyes and rolled down over her now badly swollen right cheek. The droplets hit the table top she was sitting at.
'Mum, stop. Please mum…'
'I won't stop Stacey. I can't mate. It's a mother's love. I can't just turn it off.'
Stacey now had her head in her hands and was crying as quietly as she could. Peggy though, could hear the sniffs coming from her daughter.
'Even – sniff - if I wanted to, I'll never get away alive mum. I can see that now. He'd hurt me worse than he hurt that Terry.'
'Hurt Terry? What d'ya mean they hurt him? What they done to him for gawd sake?'
Stacey winced as she realised Peggy knew nothing of the beating Terry had endured.
'Listen, he'll be alright, don't worry. Sniff – He's a bit bashed up, but he'll be ok. This time anyway. But it was a silly thing

to do mum. He looked old and slow and he looked useless. They all laughed at him. They're still laughing at him. When you speak to him, tell him to stay away from me and tell him, I'm sorry...'
'Sorry? About what? What you sorry for? Stacey!'

Then all Peggy could hear, was a dialling tone.

'STACEY!'

14.
FAMILY

Finding herself in the middle of Terry's estate, Peggy was now struggling to locate Stanhope House, the block that he lived in. Within minutes of arriving, all the concrete brick work had merged into one and everywhere looked the same. Her nerves were already jangling, and this is only making them worse. Nothing was making sense.

She then saw a senior lady in a leopard skin two piece and dangerously high heels, coming towards her. It was Elsie, who was now weighing up this new face as she approached her.
'Conservative party is it?'
Peggy was somewhat startled. She had been called many things in her life but being called a Tory was a first.
'Sorry?'
'Got your work cut out here love. Mostly Labour round here...'
Peggy suddenly felt the penny drop.
'Ah gotcha, no, no, I'm definitely not one of them love. I'm actually looking for number 11, not number 10, on Stanhope House.'
Elsie's ears pricked very quickly.
'Terry's place you mean?'
'Thats it. I'm a friend of Terry's. But not been here before. Handy you know him though.'
Elsie looked Peggy up and down further.
'Didn't think I'd seen ya round here. Known Terry long?'
A smile broke out on Peggy's face.
'You could say that yeh.'
'Funny, he's never said.'

Peggy sensed a touch of hostility and recognised it was time to

move the conversation along. She smiled at Elsie.
'Anyway, nice to meet you. I gotta be going. So, if you can point me in the right…'
Elsie on the other hand, was in no rush. She nodded towards a building to her left.
'Well, you're at the right block. I live at number 4 over there. I'm Elsie.'
She held out her right hand towards Peggy and they shook.
'I'm Peggy, as I say, nice to meet you.'
Peggy leaned back and looked up at the block
'How do I get in?'
Elsie still had hold of Peggy's hand.
'Old friend you say?'
'Yeh, sort of. If you let me, er, know how to get in? I'll let you get on Elsie.'
'S'alright. I'm in no rush, not in these shoes anyway. Only going bingo. I go with my mate Gertie from Eltham. Love me bingo me, had a fifty pound up the other night and I treated Gert to….'
Peggy felt herself getting handcuffed into a chat that she could do without.
'Listen, I'm so sorry, but I really must dash.'
Elsie also sensed some tension, so started to loosen her grip on Peggy's hand.
'...to a fish supper on the way home...'
The two of them are now staring hard at each other.
'I'm good friends with Terry meself you know, keeps an eye on me, gets me paper and that...'
Peggy finally freed her hand.
'Sorry, don't want to appear rude, but I really must go, I'm late as it is.'
Elsie grins sarcastically.
'Oh, you should have said. Well, it's easy really. Go up to the door there and press number 11 and he'll buzz you in.'

Peggy tried her best to smile, but it was getting harder by the second.
'Right, think I've got that, ta. Good luck at the bingo.'

Peggy walked over towards the intercom situated on the front entrance of the block. However, she could sense Elsie was still standing behind her, her eyes watching her like a hawk.
'Give Terry my best won't ya...lovely man…'
Peggy turned and smiled back at Elsie, nodded and muttered to herself through gritted teeth.
'and fuck Boris Johnson an' all…"
She then turned to face the block and pressed the little silver button on the box.
A distant, crackly voice was suddenly heard.
'Hello?'
'It's me.'
'Alright Peg, thought you got lost mate.'
'Here now Terry. So let me in, for gawd's sake...'
A small buzzing sound kicked in, and the main door swung open. Peggy hurried into the block. She scanned a board in front of her and saw that number 11 was on the fourth floor and she headed for the lift.

Within minutes, she was in Terry's flat. He guided her towards his front room, and she flopped onto the settee with her eyes closed. It was only when she opened them, that she realised there is another man in room.
Terry followed her in, feeling his ribs.
'Peg, meet Darren, my nephew, Tricia's kid.'
Darren reached his hand towards Peggy, nodding towards his uncle.
'Nice to meet you Peggy. I was just thinking, its funny, but I guess I'm the reason you are here today. Your email, looking for this one...'

Peggy was now more than a little flustered. She was not expecting anyone else to be there, and certainly not a well-known face off of her telly.
Peggy smiled an embarrased smlie at Darren.
'Hello Darren, yes, well yeah I guess so. Thanks for that. Sorry, you'll have to forgive me, I wasn't expecting to see anyone else here. And, sorry to hear about your mum, a lovely lady.'
Darren nodded and put his right hand over his heart.

Terry was now sat in his armchair.
'That was my idea Peg. As I said on the phone, Darren picked me up after I got the kicking, so, I've told him the full story. Drink mate?'
Peggy nodded quickly.
'Thought you'd never ask.'

Darren stood up and made his way to the table where a couple bottles of red wine, a bottle of vodka and and assortment of bottled lagers sat.
'What can I get you Peg?
Peg looked at the table,
'A glass of white if you've got one? Large…'
'Darren smiled.
'Does it come in any other size? It's in the fridge, won't be a minute.
Returning from the kitchen, with a bottle in hand, he unscrewed the cap and poured the chilled liquid into a glass.
'I'll have a lager boy.'
Peggy quickly looked at Terry.
'You mad? What with all those pain killers you're on?'
Terry grimaced.
'Ah, just the one Peg, ah go on…'

Peggy smiled as she looked carefully at Terry's swollen

features.
'Look at your poor face. You sure you're ok?'
Terry laughed her away.
'Yeh, I'm ok, mending nicely love. No real damage done. Still got my looks under all this. You alright though? Looked a bit flustered there.'
Peggy blew out her cheeks as Darren handed her, the wine.
'Ah lovely, thank you, Darren. Well, I just had the third degree off one one of your neighbours.'
Terry looked puzzled as he tried to think of who.
'Oh yeh, which one?'
'Elsie. I'd say she fancied you.'
Terry laughed loudly, before his ribs soon reminded him, that, that was a very bad idea.
'Oh, do leave off Peg.'
'I wouldn't be so sure mate. On her way to bingo, she was.'
'Oh, dear me, you'll be the talk of the 'full house Queens' tonight girl.'
Peggy took a decent sip of her wine and the cool, refreshing liquid relaxed her.
'Don't...that's all I need.'

Darren smiled as he saw Terry enjoying Peggy's company, but in truth his impatience was beginning to get the better of him.
'Don't want to appear rude here, but you ready to talk about what happened on Saturday and where we go from here?'
Peggy and Terry looked at each other and Peggy nodded towards Darren.
'Yeh, sorry Darren, actually, before we start, can I use your wotsit Terry?
'My what?'
Peggy gave him an old-fashioned stare.
Terry quickly got the picture.
Oh, the khazi… yes, turn left out of here and its two doors

down.'
Peggy walked towards the toilet and noticed a photo of a young girl in a frame on the wall. It was of her, from when she and Terry were a couple all those years ago. She stood in front of it and studied it carefully.
'Ah, bless him.'
Once finished, she quickly returned to the front room and immediately sensed an awkward silence, as Darren and Terry awaited her return.
Darren was now standing and pacing around a fair bit.
'Terry has told me the whole story and, well, sorry, but I've got to say this.
What the fuck were you thinking?'

Terry gamely tried to stand up, but he was defeated by his condition. Instead, he slumped back into his armchair.
'Oi! Who do you think you're talking to? I aint having that tone of voice aimed at her.'
Peggy felt the anger in the room, and it was the feeling she was dreading.
Darren was shaking his head.
'Well, fuck me...'
Terry once again winced as he tried to stand up quickly.
' Bollocks to it. I just told you. Behave yourself.'
Darren however was in no mood to back down.
'No, I'm not having it Terry. They could have killed you.'
Terry laughed at his nephew.
'Killed me? Oh, do leave off.'
'Look at the state of you...'
Terry suddenly felt old and useless siting there.
'Alright, alright I know, don't I. Wasn't supposed to happen like that was it? But I don't need you rubbing it in do I?'

Peggy placed her drink on the nearby coffee table and was

now facing the pair of them.
'Can you two just shut up… Please.'
Darren looked to the floor and Terry looked at Peggy and nodded.
'Thank you. Listen, I was dreading it ending up like this and in truth, I don't blame you for being like that Darren.'
Darren looked up at her.
'Like what? I think I'm being very reasonable'
Peggy held up her right index finger towards him.
'Ssshhh you for a minute. Please. Listen, I was mortified when I heard about this Darren. Sickened in fact, I never expected any of that did I?'
Her index finger now waved in the general direction of Terry's face.
Darren's eyes were now piercing directly into her eyes.
'He's an old man Peggy, he can't get involved in stuff like that...'
This time, Terry managed to get out of his chair and move towards his nephew.
'I'm not too old to give you a fucking clump, you saucy berk. Besides, SHE'S MY FUCKING KID!'

Silence enveloped the room. All three were now looking at each other.
Peggy spoke first.
'She called me. She was in tears. For what its worth Terry, she was sorry. She just had no idea who you were.'
Darren was shaking his head again.
'Peggy, this is fucking madness. She's sorry? I'd say you can tell from what happened, she ain't capable of being sorry.'
Terry was now back in his chair.
'Let's have it right, the poor mare had no idea who I was did she?'
Peggy also collapsed back back down into the sofa.

‘What did she do Terry?’
‘Eh? Nothing mate.’
Darren laughed out loud.
Peggy tried to ignore him.
‘Don’t come it, she told me to say say sorry to you, so I know she did something’
Terry just shook his head at her.

Peggy took another drink of her wine. She noticed the glass was now empty.
‘I reckon she’s ready to come home?’
Darren looked at her far from convinced
‘From what I saw in the park Peggy, it didn’t look like that would ever happen.’
Terry looked lovingly at her.
‘Why Peg?
‘Just a feeling Tel. Call it a mothers’ instinct if you want. She was really quiet on the phone, very quiet. Not giving it the big’un like she has in the past. And she sounded scared. Proper scared. Scared for her life. I think she’s finally had enough of all that.
Darren was grinning at Terry.
‘Funny way of showing it, kicking you in the bollocks...’
Peggy looked mortified
‘What? Oh my God. She never Terry?’
Terry looked angrily at his nephew.
‘You pratt…It was self preservation Peg? I was actually thinking about it in the hospital, Running scared the girl. She had no idea who I was did she? In those circumstances, I’d have done the same...’
Peggy eyes were now filled with tears. She was now totally confused.
‘What a right mess...’
‘Peg, as much as it hurts me to say it, I have to agree with

Darren. She looked like she'd never leave that mob.'
Peggy shook her head.
'She's scared for her life Tel. She told me that. She got away before and got herself into a woman's refuge place, but that Task found out where it was and broke in. He literally dragged her out of there by her hair and then battered her, I mean good and proper. She knows if she walks away again, he'll kill her this time. She knows that. Task knows she could get him killed if she talked. Not to the police, but to the rival gangs he's worried about. If she's on the loose, he'll see it as if he's in big trouble, in case she reveals his moves. He won't take that risk, letting her walk.'

Darren looked at her curiously.
'Task?' Who's that Peggy?
'The leader of that gang. A very nasty piece of work.
Terry was growing angrier by the second.
'So how do we get her out Peg?'
Darren got up and poured a botle of Peroni into a pint glasss and then topped up Peggy's wine.
'Am I hearing you right unc? You want to go back? I'm telling you, us 3 are done here. Time to get the police involved.'
Peggy drank some wine and then rested her glass on the coffee table.
'That would be fatal. First sign of the police sniffing round them Darren and they'll all disappear. We'd never find em again.'
'I'm sorry Peggy, but I can see no other way. I mean, I really can't get involved any deeper, because if this story gets out, it'll look bad on me...'
Terry looked shocked by what he just heard.
'You what son?'
Darren suddeny realised both Terry and Peggy were staring at him, obviously upset by his last comment.

‘What? Oh, come on you two. Think about it. I’ve grafted really hard to get the jobs I’m now being offered, and I’d lose all that if this got in the papers. Reports of family of mine being gang members and junkies for fucks sake. The tabloids would have a field day. It would be over for me. I mean, Terry doesn’t even really know… if she’s… his.’

Peggy slumped forward and looked down at the carpet.

‘Oh, Darren. Do you really think I’d invent all this?’
Darren suddenly felt very warm.
‘Well, you know, you knew I was doing well, had er, become famous and so you get in touch and….
Terry’s face was going redder and redder.
‘I can’t believe I’m hearing this absolute bollocks. This isn’t one of your soppy film’s son. This is real life. You really are rapidly becoming an arsehole, you know that. I knew it when I saw that fucking limo the other day. If Peg says she’s mine, she’s mine. Right? And NEVER forget where you’re from and who your family are. You hear me Darren? I got you off this estate, and away from pricks like that Task and the daily beatings, right? RIGHT! And how the fuck did I pay for that? Eh?’
Darren looked chastened. He knew he’d well and truly overstepped the mark.
‘I asked you a question son.’
‘I know, I know...’
Terry was now very riled up. He had suddenly forgotten all about his injuries.
‘Well, I thought you knew Darren, but it looks like I’m going to have to remind you. Stolen money son. The ill-gotten gains that got me fucking banged away. What would that press, that you are so worried about, make of that, eh?
Darren looked to the floor. Confusion all over his face.

'I'm sorry Terry. I wasn't thinking…'
'Listen son, I was delighted to have it to spend it on you. I didn't begrudge you a penny of it. I knew I had to get you away from the little fuckers on here, who were trying to drag you into their drugs and gangs' nonsense. Then, I hear all these years later, I have a daughter in a similar situation. And believe me, I was her once. Up to my neck in it. Fucked. Nowhere to turn. I know how that feels. And you think I'm going to do nothing? You should be ashamed of yourself son.'
Darren continued to look down, totally crestfallen.Tears could be seen slowly hitting the carpet below.
'You know what. Fuck it, while we are at it, we might as well get it all out in the open eh?'
Darren looked up at Terry and spoke very quietly
'Not now Terry...'
'No boy exactly now. If not now, when eh? Let's all go down memory fucking lane.'
Terry took a deep breath, a good drink of his lager and composed himself.
'Peg, I owe you an apology. I lied to you the other day about my Tricia. She wasn't pregnant with him when I came out.'
Darren sat and kept his head down.
'Unc, please...'
'No Peg, it wasn't like that at all. This poor little fucker, aged around three months old, was left on Tricia's doorstep by his mother, when she went back home to Newcastle. My sister found a note pinned to him saying that she, the mum, could never take a black kiddie home. So, she left him behind.'

Terry was now feeling tears in his eyes and a lump in his throat.
'A baby. She left a fucking baby, and my flesh and blood took him in… We all took him in...'
Darren lifted his head up and looked at Terry. His eyes were now bright red.

Peggy looked at Darren.
'I'm so sorry Darren, I have no idea what to say.'
Terry smiled at Darren.
'No need to say anything Peg, she loved him like he was her own. He became her own and I love him like he's my own. He simply became my nephew; he knows that I love him. But that, that is the story he doesn't want in the papers. It's got nothing to do with Stacey.'

Peggy looked at Terry, full of love.
'I know you love him, and I know you are so very proud of him. Somehow and God knows how, we're all family here right? And we're in this together, I mean who else we got?'
Darren and Terry looked at her and each other and nodded
'Good, cos am I gonna need you two, as I think I know how to get Stacey out.'
Terry wiped his eyes on an old tissue he found in his cardigan pocket.
'How Peg?'

'Money. That Task's life revolves around money. He's a greedy bastard for it. I've watched him for months now. Day in day out. Doing drug deals all day long and nicking other peoples plots from them by using casual violence. It doesn't bother him hurting people. But greed is his blind spot. Money, he's addicted to it. You can smell it coming off of him.
He'll need an incentive, cos he'll never let her go for free. But pay him enough and he'll let Stacey go and just move on. I can feel that.'

Terry nodded slowly but in truth, looked unconvinced.
'The only problem is Peg. How much is enough?'

15.
DÉJÀ VU ALL OVER AGAIN

Exactly a week after his beating, Terry felt well enough to properly leave his flat. Besides, it was Saturday morning and he had things to do.
Before making his way to the lift, he inspected his window boxes, talking quietly to the plants as he did so.
'Hello my lovelies. Sorry I aint been about. I'm back now though. I can see that Auntie Gloria has watered you, bless her, though how you poxy slugs get up here I'll never know. Trust me to have poxy SAS slugs.'
After removing a slimy creature or two and finishing a bit of deadheading, he and Daisy slowly walked over to the lift.

Emerging from the door of his block, he found he was leaning more heavily on his shopping trolley, than usual and puffing a bit as he did so. Daisy, sensing her dad was not on top form, was taking it slower than usual. Terry finally arrived at Guray's, twenty minutes later than his normal time. Guray looked at his friends face and winced.
"I heard.'
Terry smiled through his bruised face
'Nothing travels faster than bad news.'
'My customers are full of it. Saying it was that mob in the park. Fancy them having a pop at an old 'un, like......'
Terry laughed.
'Oh, I need you, don't I? Thanks for that mate.'
Guray, realising what he said, tried to style it out.
'Mate... Sorry, but you know what I mean.'
Terry smiled at his baker.
'Nah, you're alright mate. And yes, I am an old man. If I was in any doubt about that before, then I know that now for certain.'

As per every week, he paid for his rolls and bread and then made his way to Amin's to pick up his usual paper order. Before he headed back, he and Daisy took in a pit stop on a graffiti covered bench. Quite a few passers by nodded at him and he couldn't help but notice a few gossiping as they did so. Terry knew what they were talking about and also that most of it, was guess work. He just smiled. After a 10 minute breather, he was off again and heading for his block.
Having knocked at Elsie's door and getting no answer, he slowly made his way up to Dolly.
When he stepped onto the landing, he found him waiting in his doorway
'Been waiting for ya.'
He then looked Terry up and down
'Dear me, state of you. All looks a bit tender love.'
Terry rested his arm on the edge of the balcony, slowly getting his breath back.
'Smarts a bit, I won't lie Doll'
Dolly leaned in and nodded to the front door of his neighbour.
'I also saw him a couple of days ago, that Brian. He looked like a fucking panda! Two great big black eyes and a busted hooter spread all over his face. What the fuck happened to you lot?'
Terry smiled, as the recollection of Brian falling to his knees revisited him.
'It's a very long, and painful story. Got to say though, him getting a proper dig was a nice bonus. Promise I'll tell ya soon.

'Well, I'll get in a bottle scotch , ready for that big reveal.'
Terry gave out a small laugh.
'Thank you, nurse. I like the sound of that medicine. Once I'm off these heavy pain killers, I'll be straight up for a basin of that.'

Dolly smiled and kissed Terry on his bruised cheeks.
'There ya go, all better.'
Terry's last stop was on his own landing.
There, he found Elsie waiting for him with Gloria. Terry smiled when he saw them both.
'Here he comes, the walking wounded.'
'Hello Else, been looking for you love.'
'And I've been looking for you. Come here.'
She tenderly grabbed his arms and pulled his head down towards hers. Terry winced a bit as she did so, before Elsie planted a small kiss on his forehead.
'What a silly sod you are.'
Terry grinned, relieved to be out of Elsie's headlock.
'Aaah. Look at you. Come in for a cuppa Terry.'
'No Gloria, thank you, but I've got things to do, and besides, I'm knackered love.'
'Ssshh now you silly man. Get in there, you need a kit kat for five minutes.'
Terry knew he'd have no peace until he did what he was told, so he took out his deliveries for both Elsie and Gloria and left his shopping trolley on the landing. He untied Daisy from it and the pair of them then made their way into Gloria's flat. She guided him and Elsie into her front room. Terry dropped slowly into a comfy looking armchair, holding onto the arms of it as he did so, to try and soften his landing.
Gloria smiled at him.
'Now, personally I have no wish to know what happened, I'm just happy you're still here with us.'
He returned her smile.
'It's good to be here mate.'

Gloria then made her way into the kitchen to finish off making the tea. Elsie, who is also in the room suddenly winked at Terry.

‘Bollocks to that…Go on Tel, what happened? Won’t breathe a word. Old Marge said you took on 50 of them single handed…’
Terry laughed a sweet laugh her way and blew her a kiss.
‘Did she, bless her bad eyes and memory? Well, now’s not the time Else, but I promise I’ll tell ya, when I’m properly on my feet girl.’

He then looked around the walls of the room he was sat in, where every spare inch was covered by hundreds of photo frames, of every conceivable shape, size and colour. Gloria returned and placed a wooden tray on her coffee table, which sat bang in the middle of the room.
‘I was just looking at all the photos Gloria. Wonderful love.’
Gloria looked wistfully at them herself
‘Family, mostly. Though I don’t see three quarters of them if truth be told. Still, they are family…’

Elsie added two spoons of sugar from a bowl on the tray to the contents of her cup.
‘Like that now though innit, Glor. They are all over the place. Not like when we was girls. Everyone lived in the same house, next door or round the corner. Not now. Both of my two are out of London. Hardly see ‘em.’
Terry looked at his two friends and a smile broke out on his face.
‘Not got many left in my family now. Me and Darren really, what with Tricia gone.’
Gloria sadly nodded
‘I miss Tricia, a lovely lady. Still not sure how she coped back then…’
Terry looked up, as he picked up his tea-cup from the tray
‘Coped Glor?
Gloria and Elsie exchanged a glance.
‘When you were away Terry. The truth is some damn fools

on here, said some awful things to her. Funny, but that's how we all became close. With me and Elsie being a few years older, we kept an eye on her and we were bringing up our kids together, so we bonded. Didn't we Elsie?'
'We did mate and on our own too really. My old man was in the pub most of the time. Fucking hopeless case, he was.'

Gloria looked up at a photo of a young girl on her wall. Terry noticed and looked too. He guessed the girl was aged about 8 or 9. Pigtails, red gingham dress, white socks.
'My husband left after I had my second. Marcia. Thats her there. In truth, I was well shot of him. Anyway, I noticed Tricia was getting the same abuse as I was at that time. Her being called all sorts and the boy being called black this, and black that. Dog shit through the letter box, all that nonsense. Cha! Ignorant people dem.'
Terry was listening but he was struggling to take in the words.
'I should have been here for her, them. I was so stupid. Trying to be a big man. In truth I was as useless as your husbands.'
Gloria smiled at him.
'Men will always be men Terry, and women of our generation will always put the kettle on.'

Terry looked at the two of them with a lot of love in his heart.
'All I can say is, thank the Lord that you do.'
The three old mates, cups of tea in hand, then fell into a comfortable silence.

16.
SALE OF THE CENTURY

After a further week of generally taking things easy, Terry was now feeling a lot stronger and his face and body were healing nicely. That being the case, he felt well enough to call Peggy, and they were now out for a Friday afternoon stroll. Almost like homing pigeons, they found themselves heading towards Kennington Park. For Peggy going back there so soon after Terry was attacked felt a little dangerous, but Terry had reassured her he had learnt his lesson, but he also wanted to keep the pressue on Task and Stacey, by showing he wouldn't be scared off.

Upon entering the park, they soon heard a cacophony of noisy, loud voices, mixed with music blaring and dogs barking, all of which was enveloped in clouds of smoke. Peggy gripped Terry's hand tighter as the couple got nearer and nearer to the group. When they were no more than 30 foot away, Task could be seen looking their way. He whistled and most of the crowd stop talking and looked his way. He nodded at the 2 men who had given Terry the going over, and then at the couple who were now right in front of them. The 2 men walked over and stood either side of Task.

'Fuck me. You back are ya? I'll say this for you old man, you are either mad or stupid and I know what my money is on.'
He then nodded at Peggy.
'Brought back up this time I see?'
This caused a few of his rabble to laugh, more out of fear of upsetting Task, than finding the comment particularly funny. Stacey looked at Terry and Peggy almost in disbelief. She moved through those around her and stood at the front by Task.

‘Shouldn’t have come mum...’
Task looked at Stacey and then at Peggy and laughed.
‘Mum? That’s your mum? That’s mad mate. Who’s the old fella then Stace? Dad? ‘
Stacey remained quiet, putting her head down, and sensing the worst.
Terry nodded at Task.
‘You must be psychic son.’
Task smiled at him.
No! Really! Fuck me. All making sense now.
He half turned and addressed those behind him
‘Have a look. We’ve got ourselves a jolly family outing.’

Again, sarcastic laughter filled the air.
In truth, Terry turning up again, had unsettled Task and he didn’t like it. His patience was wearing very thin.
‘What you want old man? That message we left you with last time. Not clear enough for you?’
Anger had caused Task to raise his voice and this had the effect on members of the general public who were passing by, to look his way and he certainly didn’t welcome that attention.
“C’mon, speak up old man, you’re really getting on my nerves.’
Terry looked Task up and down, struggling to hide the pure disgust he felt looking at him. Task couldn’t help but sense that hatred, but just smiled at him.
Terry then looked away from Task and instead, directly at Stacey.
‘Time to come home love.’

Stacey looked at Terry with a real desperate hope in her eyes. Sensing Task looking at her, she quickkly put her head down again.
‘Listen, you silly old fucker. She aint going nowhere, you hear me.’

Terry though had seen the way Stacey looked at him and suspected Task had too.
'Aint she done enough for you? Hoisting, brassing and God knows what else.'
Stacey looked back up at Terry, having felt real, physical pain hearing him say those words. Task had seen that pain in her eyes.
'Listen, seriously, I'm in no mood for any of this. If she wanted out, trust me it would be better for me to kill her right here.'
Peggy shut her eyes as Task talked. Terry instead just smiled at Task.
'Some big man you are, eh? Another threat to hurt a bird. Bashing up old men and women, that's about your mark aint it son?'
Task's temper had fully risen now, and all this was going on too long.
'It's not a threat, it's a promise. She's useful. My best hoister, and she's got plenty of old men who would miss her.'
Terry gripped Peggy's hand tight.
'Besides, she's got a lot knowledge. If the old bill or rival associates picked her up, I'd be on offer.'

Stacey, having digested what Task had just said, looked up at him. Her body was now visibly shaking. The bruising from her last beating, was still clearly visible on her face. She spoke very quietly but they all knew she meant every word.
'I've had enough Task. I can't do this no more.'
Task smiled a gap-toothed smile.
'Back to old mum and dad is it eh? Who are you to decide that?
Stacey nodded.
'You need to know, no matter what you do to me from today, I've had enough. After today, I'm not doing anymore of this. I'm done.'

Task looked at her with bemusement.
'You know if you walk away. I'll find you and hurt you. I did it before, and trust me, I'll do it again.'
Terry reaslised this was the moment to strike.
'Listen you, its over. You can hear that. You know, we know, and she's telling you. Let her go.'

Task looked at Terry, then Stacey and then to his two right hand enforcers, who nodded his way.
'Alright, but it'll cost ya.'
Terry nodded and instinctively knew he had to play the next move carefully.
'Ok. Let's talk.'
Task walked a few paces away from Stacey and went into a huddle with his crew. There followed a lot of nodding and laughing between them.
Terry looked at Peggy, with love burning through his eyes into hers.
'We're nearly done here Peg, it'll all be over soon love.'
Task then headed back towards the couple.
'Twenty-five large. Cash.'
Terry's right eye twitched upon hearing the figure.
'You what?'
Task laughed at him
'Knew it. You heard. Too rich for your blood is it? I mean, shes only your daughter.'
Terry felt the overwhelming urge to lunge at Task, but suddenly remembered the last time he tried to do that and took a deep breath instead.
'Fuck me. Come on son, be reasonable.'
Task spat on the ground near to Terry.
'Do I look like a bloke, who has ever been reasonable? Now listen carefully. There will be no negotiations. This is simply take it, or leave it.

BUT if you leave here without agreeing, there will be no point in coming back, do I make myself clear?
She won't be here and nor will I or any of that lot behind me.'

Terry looked at the younger man in front of him and knew he was serious.
'I'll find it.'
Task laughed at him.
'Course you will. Never in doubt.'
Terry held out his hand.
'And when I pay, you leave her alone, for good. Right? That twenty-five grand, is proper 'fuck off' money.'
Task grinned at him.
'Listen you old cunt. I only want people around me, who wanna be here right. Now, get that wedge and she can fuck right off. Her leaving present to me.'
Terry nodded.
'Right, then shake on it'
Task moved closer to Terry and grabbed Terry's hand tight. Terry then returned the grip harder as he spoke.
'The people I grew up would call a handshake a contract and they never broke it. Street code.'
Task nodded.
'I know. Same in my world. Now, let go, of my fucking hand.'
Terry slowly released his grip.
'Give me a week to sort...'
Task smiled at him.
'You got two days. Meet back here, 3pm Sunday. Hand over the coin and its done. Fuck me about, and you'll have a funeral to arrange.'
A pained expression came over Terry's face.
'2 fucking days, are you sure?'

Task turned and walked away from Terry and Peggy. He

grabbed Stacey by her right arm and dragged her along. They were followed by the majority of the mob. Stacey desperately tried to look back at her mum and dad and raise her free hand. Task spoke slowly and menacingly without looking at her.

'You aint fucking gone yet slag.'

17.
WHEN SATURDAY COMES

It was approaching 7am and the day was gradually waking up. The leaves on the trees of the estate, which despite years of neglect, provided a fresh green colour among the grey and brown walls of the blocks that surrounded them.
Walking along one of the paths through the estate, Guray the baker was francticaly scanning for any sign of life. He was carrying three large white paper bags, full of freshly baked goods.

He spotted a woman on a balcony. In truth, she was hard to miss, wearing a vibrant pink towelling bathrobe, with her hair wrapped in a towel of the same hue and singing 'I'm Gonna Wash That Man Outta My Hair' at the top of her voice, as she threw a couple of black bags of rubbish down the communal chute.
'Hello! Excuse me lady. Hello!!'
Elsie looked down at the man.
'Sorry to disturb. Hope you can help me?'
Elsie's years of living in the area had given her the instinct to trust no one, especially a new face on the manor, well at least until you got to know them. So, seeing Guray, she replied very slowly, suspicion very evident in her voice.

'Possibly, wassamatta?'
Guray could feel the hostility in every syllable of that answer and so looked around for someone else to help him, but quickly realised this vision in pink was his only option. He swallowed hard.
'Ok, thank you. I'm trying find a man called Terry who lives around here. Big fella, well into his 60s, always seen with a

brown dog?'
Elsie immediately pulled her bathrobe tighter around her and looked at Guray even harder.
'And who are you that's asking?'
Guray smiled, trying his best to reassure Elsie.
'I'm the baker, Guray. I've got Terry's rolls and bread here.'
Elsie immediately relaxed.
'Ooh aint that funny. I've been looking out for him myself. He normally brings me up a couple of those rolls around now.'
Guray also relaxed, realising he was nearer to finding Terry
'That's him, same fella! That's why I'm here dear. He never misses, but there was no sign of him this morning. In truth, I'm a little worried, you know, after his recent accident.'

Elsie who quickly sensed a bit of drama and maybe a slice of fresh gossip, leant further over her balcony.
'Go to the main door down there, press number 4 and I'll buzz you in. Then get in the lift and go to the 3rd floor and wait for me. I'll meet you up there.'
Guray did as he was instructed and 5 minutes later, Elsie emerged from the same lift, and what's more she'd brought Dolly with her, resplendent in a purple silky dressing gown and fluffy and furry open toe black slippers.
'This is my neighbour Dolly. I popped in and told him about Terry.'
Guray stared at Dolly and then finally nodded a hello. Dolly nodded back.
'So, you're the roll man. Nice to meet ya. Now, from what Elsie just told me, this is not like our Terry at all, is it Mr Baker? Very much a creature of habit that one, especially on a Saturday morning.'

Upon hearing the voices on her landing, Gloria emerged from her flat. She looked a little startled at first seeing all those now

gathered outside her front door.
'Gracious…Good morning all. Thought I heard voices... '
Elsie quickly walked over Gloria
'Oooh, It's Terry Glor, he's gone missing. Wonder what could have happened to him eh? I mean you hear all sorts…'
Guray looked concerned at the way Elsie was now telling the story.
'Hello dear. Very sorry to worry you, but I'm, well, we're, looking to find him.'
Gloria looked at the white paper bags Guray was carrying and her nostrils picked up on the aroma of the still warm bread within.
'Umm, I was wondering about them...'
Elsie looked at Guray.
'Tell you what, why don't you ring his doorbell? That's him there, number 11. Go on...'
Guray swallowed hard, as he looked at the dying to know what was going on faces, all now staring his way. Gingerly, he approached Terry's front door and carefully pressed the bell.

All those on the landing, then stepped back a pace or 2 and stood in silence, trying to listen with all their collective might, for any sign of life.
They heard nothing, but silence.
After 10 seconds or so, Dolly smiled at Guray.
'Go on love, give it another prod, as I once said to an off duty chief inspector from West End central, in the Vauxhall Tavern…'
Guray, a reddening of his cheeks now very noticable, coughed lightly and pressed the bell once again.
And once again, nothing.
Dolly cupped his hands around his face as he peered through the frosted glass on Terry's front door.
'It looks very quiet…oh, hang on…I saw movement then.

Ooooh I can hear voices…sort of laughing. Blimey, someones coming...'
The chain on the back of the door could be heard being pulled back and then Terry's front door opened very slowly.
Peggy then popped her head around the now partly open door. She was barely awake and very shocked to see the crowd scene now staring back at her.
'Oh, good God…'
She suppressed a small laugh and tried to compose herself as she finally fully opened the door. She was now stood in the door frame, dressed in Terry's puffa coat and nothing else.
Elsie looked totally confused at the sight of Peggy in front of her.
'Oooh er...'
Peggy smiled at Elsie and then nodded at the others.
'Er, morning each.'
Dolly began to smile at Peggy.
'And a good morning to you too madam.'
Gloria was not entirely sure what was going on either.
'Is everything ok Peggy?'
'Yeh, Gloria, everything is, er...'

'I'm sorry missus. This is all my fault. I'm Guray the baker. Terry comes to my shop on Saturday mornings. Never misses. Only, today...'
Peggy looked at him kindly
'Yeh, hello Guray. I've heard a lot about you. Funnily enough, Terry just mentioned it was roll day. Its just that he's having, er, a bit of a lie in today.'
Dolly smiled broadly at that comment and then winked and nodded towards Gloria and Elsie. Slowly the situation became clearer to them and they too began to smile at Peggy, who at that particular second wanted to be anywhere else but standing there.

‘Look, I don’t want to appear rude, but I’m not really dressed for social calls, so...’
Dolly sensed it was time to go
‘Yeh, course love. Right. Give us the rolls here mister Guray, I’ll sort those out. Get the money to you next week love alright? Not got my purse on me at the minute…’
Guray reluctantly nodded, looking a touch confused, but he handed over the bags. Dolly then shouted over Peggy’s shoulder.
‘Ta ra then Terry love. Now remember, don’t do anything I wouldn’t do...’
Peggy managed to stifle a laugh as she then slowly shut the front door muttering to herself as she did so.

‘You’re a few hours too late with that advice Dolly, my love….’

18.
THE WIMPY BAR KID

'Not been in one of these for years. Why here?'
Darren looked around at the interior of the Wimpy Bar he was now sat in. He couldn't help but smile at the 1980s-time capsule feel of the fast-food outlet. Laminated menus stood up on formica tables which had red plastic chairs attached to them.

Terry felt slightly irritated by Darren's sneering atitutude.
'Peggy likes it here, besides, it's quiet...
Darren looked around again.
'That is a surprise...'
'Oi sarky, behave yourself, she'll be here in a minute.'
Just as he finished talking, Peggy entered, huffing and puffing as she did so.
'Sorry, buses were shocking.'
Terry got up to gave her a peck on the lips.
'No worries love, just got here ourself.
Cappuccino's all round is it?'
Peggy smiled and Darren nodded. Terry called the waiter over and they ordered their drinks.
'Alright Darren, you look well'
Already suspicious at being asked along in the first place, now with compliments coming his way, Darren was beginning to feel the 2 people now sitting opposite him, were up to something.
'Thanks Peggy, as do you mate.'
A silence then descended over the table. Eyes fleetingly looked at eyes, but no one spoke.

'Ready to order?'

That all enveloping quiet was finally broken by an eager waiter, who having delivered the cappuccinos, was now ready with his order pad.
Terry looked at the menu.
'Some right classics on here. But where are my manners. Ladies first. Darren?'
Peggy and Terry burst out laughing and even Darren had to smile.
'You cheeky uncle you. My trainer will go mad if he knows I've had this.'
'Swerve it then.'
'Are you mad unc? No, I'll have the classic burger with chips please mate.'
Terry smiled at his nephew.
'You plum. Digging it out and then can't wait to get stuck in…I'll have the same please mate. Peg?
'Ooohhh, choices…I'll have the quarter pounder with cheese, please.'
Having written down the order, the waiter was off towards the cook.

'Ok, come on then. What you invited me here for?'
Terry coughed and cleared his throat, knowing what he was about to say would cause a scene.
'Well, so, we went back yesterday and chatted to that Task fella and…'
Darren looked at them open mouthed.
'Hold on, hold on. You did what? You went to the park. Are you fucking mad?"
Peggy jumped in, tyring to stop uncle and nephew getting at each other all over again.
'We were careful love, trust me.'
Darren looked down at the tabletop and saw his hazy reflection shining back at him from the formica.

‘She’s our daughter boy. There are no options are there? Its as simple as that. We had to go back.’
Darren looked up at his uncle, who suddenly looked old and worried, two things, Darren had never seen in Terry before.
‘Turned out Peggy was right the other day. That arsehole said he’d do a deal, for the, er, right amount of money.’
Darren then slowly smiled at his uncle.
‘Oh, he did, did he.’
Terry sussed his nephew was way ahead of him.
‘Now, come on, I’ve never asked anything of you, have I? Well, HAVE I?’
Darren raised both his hands.
“Alright, alright. Easy…’
‘Well have I?’
‘No unc, no you haven’t…
Terry then took a deep breath.
‘Well, I’m about to break that rule.’
Darren smiled.
‘Thought so. Go on then. How much? What’s he after?
Peggy looked at Terry and nodded and gave him a ‘leave this to me’ smile.
‘25 grand Darren. Give him that and he’ll let Stacey walk.’

Darren could’t help but laugh at Peggy
‘25 grand. That’s a joke, right?
Terry looked at is nephew.
‘No boy. I think its fair to say that Task is not the type to go in for stand-up comedy. He said, she was a good earner, hoisting and you know, other stuff.’
Terry desperately tried to not look at Peggy as he spoke.
Darren had now stoppped smiling.
‘How do you know he’ll let her walk, once he’s paid off? How can you be sure?’
Terry rubbed his chin.

'In truth, we can't Dal, but we now have little option. Stacey was very brave and spoke up. Told him, she wanted out, so we have to move fast. We miss his deadline and he'll hurt her badly. I'm convinced of it.'
'How long you got?
'We need to get the money to him by 3pm tomorrow.'

Darren shook his head. His uncle felt some pity for him. He knew this was not Darren's fight, but he had nowhere else to turn.
'I know its a lot to ask boy, but we're fucked. You've got it, and I need it for that fucking wrong un.'
Darren looked up quickly at his uncle.
'How d'ya know I've got it?
'Well, there's that Vodafone advert you told me about, for a kick -off.'
Darren laughed out loud.
'That'll teach me…'
Peggy smiled at him.
'I know its a lot to ask love, but its family innit? While there's a chance to put it right, we've got to take it.'

Darren looked in turn at Terry and then Peggy
'Yeh, ok. Not sure I can get cash in time though, it being the weekend?'
He then saw his uncle look sternly at him
'Alright, alright. Listen, I'll sort it, I'll have a word with Moira. She'll know how to get the cash. But what happens then? Who hands it over?
'My Stacey will.'
Darren, not for the first time that lunchtime, looked confused and bafffled.
'What Peggy? Hows that work?'
'She called me last night. Checking up on me and Terry. Told

me, she'll pick the money up off us at the park gates. She said Task will test her out, to see if she'll run as soon as she gets the money.'
Darren sat there shaking his head.
'Well, I hate to say this, but he's got a point. She will. She'll have it away.'
Terry suddenly thumped the table as hard as he could, causing its contents, the salt and pepper pots and the red sauce container shaped like a tomato to tumble over. Coffee had now also been spilt into saucers.
'Will she fuck, you berk. Aint you worked it out yet? She's had enough.'
Peggy stood the tomato upright and then grabbed the left hand of Terry.
'It's time to trust her Darren. I know, she'll hand over the money and then walk away with us. If Im wrong I'll walk out of your lives and believe me, that's the last thing I want to do right now.'

Darren smiled ironically at the two old people, now in front of him.
'Look, I know its fucking tough for you two, but this is, madness…'
Terry nodded and he smiled back at his nephew.
'Well, maybe you're right. Maybe it is madness. But its too late anyway son. We've told him, he'll get his money. We shook hands, me and him and he understood what that means. I could see it in his eyes.'

Darren pulled his dark green baseball cap down over his eyes, contemplating what to do next.
'Alright. Fuck it. Ok.' But, as it's my money, I do it my way. I'll take it to her. I'll go with my driver Simon, so if it gets heavy...'

Peggy immediately looked concerned
'No love, we can't have that. It'll get really messy. Tell him Terry…'
Darren jumped back in.
'Hold on Peggy, please. If its all about trust now, then its time to trust me too. I'll take it to her and will only call Simon if I have to. Think of him as my back up.'
Peggy looked very worried.
'But I've told Stacey it'll be me and your uncle...'
Darren was in no mood for a discussion.
'Just let me know the meet details. It will be fine, I'm telling you, right?'
Terry finished off his coffee and then sat back in his chair.
'Thought you didn't want to get too involved though son?'
Darren stood up and pulled on his navy-coloured quilted waistcoat, just as the waiter arrived with their food order.

'In truth, I don't. But I'd say it was 25 grand too late to think like that now unc, wouldn't you?'

19.
THE PAST BECOMES YOUR FUTURE

It was 2.50pm on Sunday and Stacey was standing outside the main gates of the park, opposite Kennington Road. Her eyes were darting left and right scanning the pavement in front of her for any sign of Peggy and Terry. She was flanked by Chugs and Grim, Task's most trusted men. They too are scanning around them for a grey-haired couple.

'Stacey? Right?'
Suddenly, a mixed-race guy around the same age as Stacey is standing right in front of her. She looked up at his face but didn't recognise him.
'Got the wrong bird mate. Now, do yourself a favour and fuck off will ya.'
Darren looked down at her.
'Listen, I aint trying to pick you...'
Stacey was about to launch into him, and then Darren noticed one of the two men standing near her, move threateningly towards him.
Darren quickly held up both his arms.
'Hold on, hold on, easy chaps, easy...it's ok. I'm from her mum and dad. I have got the right Stacey, haven't I? If its you, I've got your transfer fee in here.'
He nodded at a yellow Selfridges carrier bag he was carrying on his right shoulder.

Stacey looked hard at him puzzled.
'Before I answer that, just who the fuck are you?'
Darren smiled.

‘Darren, Terry’s nephew.’

Chugs, then moved in so close, his nose was almost touching Darren’s.
‘You aint what we were told to expect. This deal is dead. Now fuck right off, before I burst ya.’
Darren could smell the skunk fumes emanating off the lump now in front of him and they were getting down the back of his throat. He also knew this was going all wrong, before it got started. He knew he had to stay calm.
‘Fuck me, hang on, hang on. Her mum has been taken ill. All the stress of this, her GP reckons.’
Stacey’s eyes immediately teared up.
‘Ill? How ill? How bad is she?’
Darren looked at Stacey and noticed her face, which after all the years of neglect and rough and battered skin, looked pretty normal. She was quite pretty actually and instinctively he couldn’t help but feel a little sorry for her.
‘Don’t worry, mum’s going be fine. Her nerves are bad that’s all. Terry called me. He said he wanted to stay with her, make sure she was alright and for me to get the money to Stacey. So, here I am.’
Stacey looked at the muscle towering over her, and it nodded at her

‘Ok, give me that bag. My favourite shop that by the way, so good choice. You wait here.’
Darren looked concerned. Fear coursed through his entire body.
‘No, no, hang on.’
Stacey reached out for the bag.
‘Time to trust me new boy. Come on, hand it over. You stay here though, right?’
Darren hesitated, but realised he had little option but to do

what he had been told.
Stacey turned and walked off with Chugs and Grim and headed towards Task. Chugs called ahead to explain what was happening. Darren, looking at them moving away from him noticed a tall-ish man up ahead, take the call.

As Stacey approached Task, he eyed her suspiciously. He also looked behind her and at Chugs.
'What's this bullshit about a no show from Ma and Pa Walton then?'
'As I said, this new face turned up. Said he was a nephew. He said, the old lady is ill, so he says he's the courier, that's him back there.'
Chugs nodded back to Darren, who was still at the park gates, as he was told, a good 100 feet away.
Task looked at the Selfirdges bag that Stacey was carrying. He grabbed it from her and handed to Chugs.
'Count it.'

Stacey looked directly at Task.
'That's it. I'm done Task. I'm tired mate. Tired of the nicking for you, fucking sweaty old men for you, and taking the junk I have to take because of you. But most of all, I'm tired of you. Time for me to go.'
Task looked at her and laughed.
'Is that fucking right. Well, even if the money in that bag adds up, you aint going nowhere. You're staying. Final word.'
A burning rage welled up in Stacey and she no longer cared what happened to her.
'Nah, you cunt. You absolute, fucking cunt. I'm going mate. I'd rather be dead than work for you anymore. You and this way of life, my way of life, disgusts me…'

Bang!

Task suddenly hit her hard across her face with a clenched fist. Stacey stumbled backwards and fell onto her arse. The right-hand side face cheek was now stinging like crazy, and a thin trickle of blood emerged from her nose.
Task was now fixated on her, looking down and getting ready to hit her again.
'You carry on talking like you're fucking talking, you no good two bob slag and I'll kill you right here and now.'
Stacey flinched, getting ready for the next blow, but as she did so, she saw Darren walking fast and then running towards them. She wasn't the only one that had seen him. Grim was now trying to catch Task's attention.
'Boss, BOSS! Look!'
Task looked at Grim and then towards where he was looking and then smiled.
'Oh good, here comes the cavalry.'
Darren got within 6 foot of Task, before he was headed off by 3 others who had been standing behind Task, who now looked directly at Darren.
'And what the fuck do you want?'
Darren stared directly back at Task and studied his features very closely before speaking.
'I'll tell you want I don't fucking want, and that's damaged goods. What you hitting her for?'

As he was about to answer, Task noticed Chugs giving him the thumbs up regarding what was in the Selfridges bag.
'Got fuck all to do with you, what I do with her, courier bwoy. As for you getting damaged goods, no need to worry about that. No, no, no. Cos she aint going anywhere. Now fuck right off.'
The mob behind their boss began laughing, jeering and making all sorts of gestures towards Darren, who just smiled back at them.

'Is that your final word… Jeremy?'
Task looked hard at Darren.
'That is you Jeremy, isnt it?'
Task's mob looked quizzically at each other.
Stacey then stood up and looked at Darren,
'What you calling him Jeremy for?'
'Why? Because that's his name Stacey, or it was when I last saw him. Jeremy… Cargill. Back then, he was head of a little firm called The Awakening. They terrorised most of the estate I grew up on, me included.'

Stacey started to laugh quietly in the face of Task.
'Fucking Jeremy. You know what, it suits you.'
Task raised his right arm, about to strike Stacey again, only Darren caught his arm on its downward path. He looked at Task and shook his head.
Task looked at Darren closely and grinned at him.
'Well, for what it is worth, I don't remember you one fucking bit. You would be just one of hundreds of nuisances I dealt with. And that name you're using. That name is in my past. All the people who called me that, are dead. Natural or otherwise. Only you left using it.'

Darren still had a grip of Task's wrist.
'I've noticed recently, our past, has a way of catching up with us. As you don't remember me, perhaps I should remind you. You truly fucked me over back then, scared the life out of me. But good, strong people, saved me. And then today, I'm back in your face, only bigger, stronger and older.
Darren then looked at Stacey.
'See her? She leaves here today. Her dad shook your hand. That's a done deal. Even a complete arsehole like you knows that.'

Task took off his camoflague puffa jacket and started to circle Darren aggresively.
'We'll see about that. Me and you. Winner takes all. Her and the cash. What you say delivery bwoy?'
Darren could feel the eyes of all around, boring into him. He knew he could't back down.
'Like that is it Jeremy? '
Suddeny Chugs, steps between them.
"Fucking brick shit house coming right this way and fast.'
Darren doesn't turn around; he knows who it is.
Task looked over at Simon who was getting closer all time and then, he was at Darren's side.'
'Boss, out of there. I'll handle this.'
Darren began to take off his navy quilted coat.
'Really good to see you mate, but I'm having this one. Hold that will ya?'
Simon reluctantly took the coat from Darren.

Task suddenly fell to the floor and with his stiff leg, swept into the feet of Darren, which had the effect of making him lose his balance and fall to the floor. Immediately the mob closed in and surrounded the two of them, forming a ring. Task, got a swift kick into Darrens ribs as he lay there and then aimed a kick at Darren's head. Sharply though, Darren caught Task's foot and managed to propel him backwards and he ended up on his arse. Darren was up quick and got a hard, swift kick into Task's bollocks, which winded him badly. Somehow, Task staggered to his feet and then slowly took up a boxing stance. Darren did the same and then surprised Task with his hand speed and weight of punch, as he landed a couple of hefty jabs on Task's nose and right eye. Darren then crouched down and hits Task with a solid right-hand to his ribs.

The blood that Task can now feel flowing from around his

right eye, riled him and he reached down under his right trouser leg, pulling out a large sharpened screwdriver. He then flashed that past Darren's face a couple of times. On the third pass, it sliced a 6-inch gash on Darren's cheek. Task was now thrusting the tool forward like a knife. Darren was quick with his evasive moves to avoid it and then managed to knock the hand carrying the screwdriver upwards, causing Task to lose grip of it.

Simon quickly picked up the screwdriver, and he lobbed it towards Darren. Grim was now walking towards Darren, carrying a knife, which he'd been passed by one of the mob behind him. Darren was up on his toes and despite now struggling a little for breath and feeling a stinging in his cheek, he continued to goad Task.
'I see nothings… changed… then Jeremy…You always did… like the odds…stacked in your….favour.'
Task was as equally short of breath and shocked at how well Darren has stood up to him.
'Fuck you… no rules…never has been.'
Grim suddenly charged in from Darren's right hand side, but as he did so he is rugby tackled to the ground by Simon, who then quickly thrusts the open palm of his right hand under Grim's chin and a sharp cracking noise is heard.

'Woah!'

A cry goes up from Task's mob, some of whom are filming what is taking place in front of them, as are around 50 members of the public.
Grim fell to the ground, unconscious. Simon calmly picked up the knife. Task is now skipping backwards from Darren and he slipped. He was now on the ground. Darren walked slowly towards him and then knelt down, with both of his

knees pinning Task's arms to the concrete.
Darren's left hand was around Task's throat and he had the screwdriver raised above Task's head.
Task's right eye was closed and his head and body flinching, as he awaited the next blow.

Suddenly, the gathering gloom of the dark early evening was bathed in blue flashing light as a couple of police cars, and then a van screeched up outside the park, their sirens blaring. Police officers jumped from the vehicles and began to run round the railings, heading towards the nearest entry gate. One of the mob, black hoodie pulled up over his head, broke free from the rest and grabbed the Selfridges bag from the hand of Chugs.
'Chip! chip for fucks sake.'
Bodies from the mob and the public, scatter into the dark of the park, franctically searching for the various exits. Task having heard the sirens, has opened his right eye and is looking at Darren.
'Have her. Fucks sake have her. She means fuck all to me.'
He then turned his head to look directly at Stacey and hissed at her.
'You know, you look really old girl. Used up. Rinsed. It was fucking time to retire you anyway...'
Darren jumped up, and off Task's arms. Task got up slowly and without another word, walked calmly into the shadows. Stacey was trying to take deep breaths, between heavy sobs. Tears rolled down her cheeks, through a combination of fear and sheer relief. Her body was shaking uncontrollably.
A couple of police run up to Darren and grabbed him whiilst he was still holding the screwdriver. He immediatley dropped it to the ground .
'All cool here boss, all cool…'
The police ignored Darren, taking no chances and they soon

have him bent over one of the table tennis tables. As they search his pockets, Simon walked up to a senior copper and began to tell him what had occurred and who Darren was.

Darren was then turned round and told to stand up straight as his hands were bound together with heavy duty black cable ties. Stacey caught his eye as he was being body searched.

He looked straight back at her and smiled broadly.
She then slowly, smiled back towards him.

20.
SANCTUARY

A few days later, Terry was up and out of his flat early. As arranged, he dropped Daisy off at Elsie's for the day, having told her he had some important business to deal with in town, and the dog couldn't come. From Elsie's, he got a bus to Victoria train station and from there, he alighted at East Croydon. He then picked up a cab from outside the station. Sitting in the back seat, he suddenly felt very anxious and nervous. He knew he had definitely left his comfort zone and then some.
The cab driver delivered him outside the address, Terry had given him. Terry paid the fella and then climbed out and had a good look at the building in front of him. Whispering out loud, he began telling himself to relax. He took in gulps of air in deep breaths. This had the effect of slowing down his heart rate and sort of calmed his shaking hands.

'Here goes then…'
He blew the excess air out of his cheeks and his right index finger pressed the doorbell in front of him. After what seemed like minutes, but in reality, was only 30 seconds, Peggy opened the door.
She was looking flustered.
'Am I pleased to see you love. Come in.'
As Terry entered her house, Peggy reached up and kissed him on the cheek. He in return, gave her a long soft hug.
'You look tired girl. I can see it's been tough.'
Peggy could feel that Terry was shaking while they hugged.
'Yeah, you could say that. The poor kid aint half going through it, Tel. Sickness, diarrhoea, crippling headaches, stomach cramps, the lot. She's also said, just about everything aches. She's also hallucinating something terrible. Keeps saying

something about a black tar pit in her stomach, and her reaching down into it and trying to get something out. Horrible, and it seems like it's on repeat that. I was just clearing up her sick bucket, when you rang the bell. I've just got her settled again. Give it ten minutes and I'll take you up.'

Terry nodded and then looked round the nicely decorated hallway. He looked very puzzled.
'You alright Terry? I could feel you shaking then.'
Terry shook his head, half smiling.
'I'm alright Peg, just a bit worried. Nervous, I guess? I'll be ok mate. I just want to get this right. She's my kid and I want to make it all right.'
Terry then began looking around once again.
Peggy couldn't help but notice the puzzled look on his face.
'What are you looking for?
'Your kitchen. Was gonna put the kettle on. Think we both could do with a cuppa eh? '
Peggy smiled at him.
'Listen, you're a good man Terry Williams. You know that? Just you being here today, will mean the world to that girl. So please, stop looking so worried. It'll all be fine, you hear me. The second she walked out of that, that rubbish; her life was back on track and we'll make sure it stays that way.'

Terry looked down at her smiling and sighed. He was slowly beginning to feel at ease for the first time since he walked through the front door. He then leant down and kissed Peggy on the lips and they hugged.
'Right, what you fancy? Tea of coffee? I might even try and rustle up some biscuits…'
Peggy smiled.
'Oh, will ya, you cheeky sod. Go on then, I'll have a nice cup of tea love ta. The biscuit barrel is next to the toaster. You sort

that and I'll go and check on Stace.'

Peggy then made her way up the stairs and Terry began opening the white drawers and doors that made up the kitchen cabinets, looking for cups, spoons and teabags etc.
Five minutes later, Peggy was back in the kitchen . Terry handed her a cup of tea.
'Oooh ta love. I could murder that. Stace said give her a few minutes and you can go up and say hello.
Suddenly, Terry's waves of anxitety returned.
'You sure? I mean, I'd love to, but I dont want to upset her or...'
Peggy placed her right hand on his right hand.
'You'll be fine love. Stop worrying, she cheered right up when I told her you were here. I even got a little smile. You pop up and say hello . She's ok honest. There's still a lot to do, but she's better each day.'

Terry sipped his coffee and then noticed his reflection in a mirror situated in Peggy's dining room. He walked over towards it and then studied the man now looking back at him.
'Fuck me, I look old. I almost don't recognise myself.'
Once again, he puffed out his cheeks,
'And I wasn't this nervous, going in front of that Chocolate who put me down for that stretch all those years ago.'
Peggy took his coffee cup off him and placed it on a nearby table.
'Enough stalling. Go on, up you go. It's the second door on the right. I'll be right behind you, but I'll leave you two to have a chat. I'll be just outside if needed.'

Terry checked his reflection once again and then turned and began the climb up the stairs. Once he had reached the correct door, he gently tapped upon it. There was no answer. He

waited a few sconds and then knocked again, a little harder the second time. He then heard a weak voice coming from behind the door.
'Hello. That you Terry?'
He gently opened the door a few inches and then looked in.
'Yes love, it's me Terry...Dad…'

Stacey smiled upon hearing his voice and slowly lifted her head up off her plain white pillow. Terry couldn't help but notice her face was almost the same colour. She tried to speak, but her throat was dry, and her words just turned to dust. She then reached out her right arm from under her white duvet and sipped a small amount of water, from a glass tumbler on her bedside cabinet.
She then tried to speak again.
'Hello Terry, that's better, thanks so much for coming. It really is lovely to see you. I know my mum was missing you.'
Terry looked lovingly at his daughter.
'It's lovely to see you both too. Mum was telling me you're having a rough time of it love. It will get easier mate. Promise.'

Stacey smiled as best she could.

'Soon, I hope. I'm only just about keeping that water down. I feel like I've been in a tumble dryer for a week. My heads all over the shop. I was dreaming then that I was a text message being sent from one mobile phone to another and I couldn't stop it or get out.'
Terry looked at her with all the love he could muster.
'That sounds horrible. Remember, it's just your body and mind testing you Stacey. It's bound to be strange for the first week, ten days, I guess. But it'll get easier. And we both know yov've got the best nurse in the whole world looking after you. She'll sort you out.'

Tears began to trickle down Stacey's cheeks.
'Shes been amazing - snifff - when I think of the trouble and grief, I put her through -sniff - I feel so ashamed of myself.'
Terry felt his eyes welling up too.
'It's a mothers love girl. Stronger than dyanmite that.'
He then sat on the end of the Stacey's bed.
'She is one remarkable woman. When she told me about her having you, my mind nearly exploded. I could have honestly crawled into a hole in the ground and died in there. The fact that I was banged up, while she carried you and then brought you up, when I knew nothing about it, well it crucified me. I was such a stupid fucking idiot. And then, my heart swelled to twice its normal size, when I found out I had a daughter. It's a miracle.

Stacey looked lovingly at him.
'Listen, when I get over this, we'll all start again. We'll rebuild it, all of us. Proper family stuff . We've still got time.'
Peggy was sitting down on a small wooden chair in the passage by the room, and quietly wept as she listened to them both talking.
Terry reached out his hand and Stacey did the same.
'Thats all I want girl. For us to get to know each other and be a family. It's so wonderful now knowing I have you. I'll be honest, I'd given up on life really. I was tired and just fed up with people. The majority just drove me mad, so I avoided them and withdrew into my own little word. And then, this. Your mum, and you, come back into my life and I suddenly feel like I'm alive again. In truth, I never stopped loving your mum, and then to have you, well, its so special.'

Stacey smiled at him, but he could see she was struggling to keep her eyes open. She was beginning to drift in and out of consciousness, as waves of tiredness came crashing into her.

Terry got up off the bed, the movement of which made Stacey stir.
'Listen love, I can see you are tired. You get some kip and I'll be back soon. I promise you that'
Stacey slowly opend her eyes and beckoned him closer.
'Dad. Before you go. Give us a kiss.'
Her voice was so quiet, that Terry could barely hear her. She smiled at him as he hesitated.
'Come on you, do as you're told.'
Terry slowly walked around the bed and towards her and then bent his head towards hers. He carefully and lovingly, kissed her on the forehead and they both smiled.
Stacey, then laid her head down into her pillow and a peace came over her face, as she drifted off to sleep.

Terry carefully crept out the room and immediately fell into the arms of Peggy, who was now standing up by the bedroom door. Terry then gently whispered.
'She's having a sleep. She's soundo. I'll come down for half hour and we can have a catch up eh?
Peggy gripped him tighter and held onto him for a minute or so, as they both wept tears of joy, sadness, but ultimately, hope, all wrapped into one.
They made their way downstairs and into the dining room and each sat down, drying their eyes on white paper tissues, plucked out of a small square box, sat on the dining room table.

'She'll be alright won't she Peg? I mean, long term.'
Peggy smiled at him.
'Yeh, she'll be ok. She just needs looking after and then she'll be right as ninepence. My GP came round a couple of days back and gave her the once over. She said that despite her lifestyle for the last 20 years, Stacey was doing well really. She said, she just needs a bit of pampering and love.'

Terry smiled.
'Well, we've got plenty of that aint we? Listen, I'm gonna shoot off and let you two get some rest. But before I do, do you need any shopping? I can easily shoot round Tesco's or whatever you got out here.'
Peggy smiled as she yawned a tired old yawn.
'Oh, hark at me. Blimey. Thanks love, but we're fine actually. Your Darren has been in every evening since she came home, and he's brought in all we need. Him and Stacey seem to be getting on really well.'

Terry looked surprised and then smiled.
'Has he? The rascal? I've not seen a lot of him recently, told me he was busy, but when I have, he's never really mentioned about what happpened in the park and definitely nothing about coming here?'
'I'm sure he'll talk to you soon enough. When he's ready. He's told me, when Stacey's fit enough, he's taking her to a spa down in Suffolk to get away from London for a while. Sounded like, he's got it all worked out.'
Terry smiled and looked puzzled at the same time.
'Blimey, what a turn up.'
Peggy smiled at him and then they both laughed for the first time in quite a few days.

21.
HOME

THREE MONTHS LATER

Terry breathed in the early morning fresh air as he stepped out of his front door with Daisy by his side. He stopped on his balcony to check on his flowers in their window boxes and tubs. His large navy coloured towelling bath robe flapped in the breeze, as he wandered around, saying good morning to the plants. Peggy come to the door frame and watched her man in silence, as the greenery in front of him, pleasantly distracted his mind and within minutes, he could have been anywhere in the world.
'Ten minutes Monty Don, then in for a wash and brush up, you hear me?'
Terry smiled as he turned and blew Peggy a kiss, before picking up his green plastic watering can and setting to work.

A couple of hours later, Terry and Peggy were dressed and ready for the guests they were excitedly expecting. The flat smelt of a roast chicken dinner that Peggy had prepared. Daisy was sat in a corner already licking her lips, dreaming of any leftovers. Terry and Peggy were sat in silence, both feeling a litle nervous. Terry suddenly looked lovingly at Peggy.
'You look lovely mate. Really smart.'
Peggy smiled at Terry.
'Scrubbed up well yourself sir. Glad we got you out of that bath robe and away from Kew Gardens out there'

Ding Dong!

Terry nearly jumped out of his skin as the doorbell told them their guests had arrived. He got up as quick as his old bones would allow and opened the front door to reveal Darren and Stacey looking back at him, both looking the picture of health. They were both dressed in predominantly white and tanned and they positively glowed.

‘Wow! Look at the pair of youse. Peg, PEG! Here mate, have a look at these two will ya.’
Peggy walked up the passage and she and Stacey immediately fell into an embrace. Terry shook Darren’s hand and then pulled him in closer for a hug.
‘Come here son, I’m so proud of ya…’
All went quiet for a few seconds as they hugged, kissed and swapped places. Not wanting to be left out, Daisy stood up on her hind legs and yapped away and danced around, excitedly. Finally, they all separated and made their way into the front room.
‘Drink Dal?’ Wine or beer?’ Stace?
Peggy shot a sharp look at Terry.
‘I won’t Terry, just a sparkling water for me. Besides, I’m still on my tablets and thankfully, I don’t fancy one.’
Terry was crestfallen. He put his hands to his head.
‘I’m so sorry Stacey, I’m so bloody clumsy.’
Stacey walked over to him and grabbed his hand.
‘Don’t be so silly dad. No damage done. No need to worry about me. Drink never did do me any favours. I won’t miss it mate.’

Hearing the word dad, hit Terry hard right into his heart. Peggy watched the tears well up in his eyes, as they did in hers. Stacey couldn’t help but notice the pair of them.
‘Stop it you two, or you’ll have us all at it.’
Peggy looked at her daughter and broke out into the widest of grins.

'Just look at you. You look so well love.'
They got up and cuddled again. Peggy kissed Stacey's face.
Darren poured some lager from a bottle into a glass, he has just been handed by Terry. He then raised it to his uncle. Terry returned the gesture with his red wine.
'Great to see you boy'
'And you unc.'

'So, Suffolk. It was good to hear from your Simon that you arived safe and well.'
Darren looked over at Peggy.
'Yeh, the ideal spot. Just seemed best to get Stacey away from it all for a bit once she was well enough.'
Peggy smiled.
'I asked Simon about what happened in the park, but bless him, he didn't say too much, only that all that training you were doing in the gym for that part, paid off nicely.'
Darren laughed, and for the first time, Terry noticed the small scar on his nephew's face.
'Waasat?"
Darren gently rubbed the wound.
'Honestly unc, it's nothing. Just a scratch.
Stacey left the embrace of Peggy and sat down next to Darren and took a sip of her water.

'You would have been proud of your boy dad. He gave old Jeremy a proper run for that money.'
Terry looked puzzled.
'Jeremy? Who's he when he's at home?
Stacey and Darren both laughed.
'Ah it's a long story unc. Let's just say, he was a face from our past and I dealt with it. I'll tell you the rest one day soon, but I'm having no negativity in here today.'
Stacey then linked arms with Darren.

‘Suffolk was great. Darren found a great rehab place down there, and we had an Airbnb near to that. I went every weekday, whilst Darren worked out in a local gym and read his script getting ready for that action film he’s got coming up. We’d meet at the end of my day and ate good food and rested up really. Did me the world of good. I also started to get a few things sorted out, like that stupid tattoo lasered off my hand, and I started to get my teeth fixed, look!
Stacey proudly showed of her temporary dental work.
‘First thing I noticed when you came Stace, they look great.’
Thanks mum, I’ll get out to Turkey, once my passport comes in and get them sorted properly. ’

Darren then smiled at Stacey.
‘We also did a lot of talking down there, as we didn’t know each other that well really. I told Stacey my story of growing up and how Terry and mum took me in, and she explained what happened to her, and how easy it is to get lost in that world. I guess we’re both damaged goods in many ways, but somehow, we’ve come through tough times and now, well, we’ve found each other. We know its day to day, but it’s going really well. We’ve got close, as we said on our texts. None of that was planned, but you know…’
Terry noticed a reddening on Darren’s face.
‘I think you’re blushing boy’
‘Nah, nah, unc, you’ve got the heating on high’
The marvellous sound of laughter then broke out among them all.

Stacey gazed lovingly at her mum
‘You know this, all this, its all down to you mum.’
Peggy smiled and nodded at her daughter.
‘I don’t know why, but I just knew you were ready to come home love?’

Terry took a decent sip of his red wine.
'Well, I've never seen Peg so happy. She's even been going bingo with Elsie and her mate Gert!'
Peggy threw the tea towel she was carrying at Terry.
'Oooh you sod!'
Stacey laughed and then looked reflective as she caressed Peggy's hands.
'I've still got a bit of a way to go mum, but the past 20 years, already seems like a different lifetime. It's like it never happened. I know I've been so lucky.'
She looked over to a smiling Darren.
'And I'm super proud of him.'

Terry noticed Peggy had stared off into the middle distance, seemingly lost in her own world of thoughts.
'You alright Peg?'
His voice broke her trance.
'Sorry mate, I was miles away. Just thinking of how life can change so quickly. One thing I've really learnt over the last few months is that money can't buy what I'm feeling right now, and that's love.
At the end of the day, I reckon that is all any of us really need.'

The End.

THE EPILOGUE

Embracing the Decline.

The barnet's going
The minces too
Your mouth nowadays, has a lot less teeth
And definitely more glue

Sure, the hair can make a comeback
And the railings can be fixed
Some look great by doing that
Most, pickled in aspic

The waist band on your strides is creaking
They appear to have somehow, shrunk
Your six-pint days have now long gone
A shandy, leaves you drunk

Not out as much, as you once were
It's my knees you cry, done in
So now, you pick your battles carefully
But battles, you can win

Good people ask, how you are doing
Fine you say, just fine
Don't you worry about me, my son
I'm embracing the decline

We know it could be so much worse
At least we are still here
Ones we loved, have left, and gone
No more, from them, we hear

Memories, are still held close
Now bizarrely on our phone
It used to be in photo albums
Those days, revved up, and gone

I sometimes wonder, what my old man would say
If I said, come here, and look
At the world I now inhabit
On a thing that's called Facebook

He'd call me a plum and say, 'grow up,
Life needs living, not uploaded'
He'd be right of course, and I wonder how
We all ended up, barcoded

One last beef before I chip
And that's on today's clothing
Trainers, Lycra, and track suits
Dressed for comfort, posing.

A rant of an old man? Maybe so
My time gone? Best you save that bet
My clock is ticking, loud, and clear
But there's life in the old dog yet

So, when you're asked, how you have been
Tell them, fine, just fine
Don't you worry about me, treacle
I'm embracing the decline.